I0520357

the mystery of
Wycliff
Manor

John Lars
ZWERENZ

Green Frog Publishing • East Montpelier, VT 05651

The Mystery of Wycliff Manor

by John Lars Zwerenz

Green Frog Publishing
P.O. Box 46
East Montpelier, VT 05651

First Edition
Written by John Lars Zwerenz
Edited by Cecilia Bizzoco
Cover design and layout by Green Frog Publishing

Cheers for reading this copyright page! Most readers don't bother. To reward your efforts, here is a new word that you won't find elsewhere in this book. Use this word to amaze your family and friends with your improved command of the English language!

Requiem: noun, (1) : a mass for the dead, (2a) : a solemn chant (such as a dirge) for the repose of the dead, (2b) : something that resembles such a solemn chant, (3a) : a musical setting of the mass for the dead, (3b) : a musical composition in honor of the dead. Many thanks to Merriam-Webster, accessed April 14, 2023.

ISBN 978-1-7344600-8-7
Library of Congress   2023907851

Prepared, printed, and bound in the United States of America.

To Mary, Queen of Angels

Table of Contents

Introduction

The Mystery of Wycliff Manor was penned with a gravely important eschatological meaning in my mind for all its prospective readers. This story was deliberately conceived and crafted to serve as a solemn warning to all readers who come across this book that grave, evil deeds, unrepentant, will lead to eternal loss. In ontological existence, there is indeed the reality of an eternal place of everlasting punishment for unrepentant souls who die in a state of mortal sin. This novel is direct and simple in expressing that absolute and objective truth.

Wycliff Manor uses its specific story in which I espouse the correlative horrors of this truth in detail to emphasize the sobering and stark reality of eternal damnation for the gravely serious and persistent sinner. In writing this book, I became ever more aware and edified in the undeniable realities of the darkest realms of moral justice.

Throughout the history of humanity, evil deeds have, like a corrosive thread, corrupted the goodness which God first instilled within the soul of man. At times this evil has found its way into vortexes of certain physical and intangible places where malevolent forces have made their home, reign supreme and unchallenged. Wycliff Manor is such a place. And if anyone doubts that a single house can be entirely given over to all things evil, let him read on.   ✟

But he knoweth not that the dead are there;
and that her guests are in the depths of hell."

Proverbs 9:18

At the foot of a castle in the gilded, setting sun,
In the warm and fragrant air of a Summer's belvedere,
Through a deep, dense forest a river did run
Winnowing through the trees, azure hued and clear.

And in the languorous night, when stars appeared like wines,
As harbingers of autumn, in the dusky, turquoise sky
A maiden of regalia, from epochs long gone by
Walked out upon the terrace, gazing at the pines.

Her flowing, blonde mane was lovely, long and fair
And her royal gaze was of the sacred night
When songbirds sang in the sad moonlight
Above the many fountains, rising in the square.

Chapter One
Massachusetts

James Asher, Junior was a man generally known for his rigorous austerity and unflinching discipline. Yet when the wine was to his taste, and his dinner company consisted of old, familiar friends, something genuinely warm beamed from his countenance.

James was a twenty-five-year-old post-graduate student at Harvard University in Boston. He was a talented scholar with an impressive semblance of morality, intelligence, physique, and aesthetics.

It was early spring 2021, and James was driving his new car on a small and rustic peninsula over a narrow dirt road in the eastern extremity of Martha's Vineyard. Darkness consumed the wild sky, and a tremendous rumbling borne of thunder could be heard miles away.

James continued driving to a relatively quiet place next

to an inlet that opened to the sea. After parking, he left his blue Chevrolet and walked in his cowboy boots to the cusp of the surf on the sandy floor.

Gazing to the east, he looked far out upon the Atlantic Ocean. James could not help but smile.

Two weeks later, in a small cafe in Beacon Hill, after one last sip of black coffee, he called on the waitress who had served him to ask for his check. It was April, and James was in the process of attaining his doctorate in archaeology.

He paid for his meal with cash and, rising somewhat hastily from his table, he began the rather short walk to Boston Common, his favorite place to ponder life, as well as to study. To graduate with a Ph.D., James was required to write an extensive dissertation in relation to his specialized field of study, which was the impact on economics in times of war and their effect on archeological findings.

He arrived at The Common as the sun was setting, expanding as it descended with livid hues of lavenders, violets, and bright orange-tinted clouds of gold. James' preferred place to sit at The Common was next to a pond in the heart of the park on an old oak bench. His leather boots rested in tall, slender grass as his tranquil gazes would serenely overlook the water's surface. His head would often be fanned there by expansive boughs with emerald leaves like giant feathers hovering high over his brow.

As he would rest, meditate, or study, James could sometimes hear distant music echoing from the Parkman Bandstand on the eastern side of The Common. That day, as he sat half asleep on his favorite bench, James could hear the pacifying strains of Mozart's Clarinet Concerto in A minor.

Two hours passed, and unaware, James had fallen asleep. As daylight began to morph into dusk over the great city of Boston, James became aware of a burgeoning darkness in the sky. A thick, dark fog from the Charles River basin had been slowly crawling south, expanding as it began to cover the entire grounds of The Common.

An oppressive sense of thunder with sprawling gray clouds cloaked the now hidden, dying sun. Some profound presage of danger seemed to amass in the dark gray firmament. James seemed to perceive an amorphous yet stern warning in the sky, a malevolent harbinger of some pernicious evil that awaited him.

Just as he made the decision to hurry home, he noticed the rain. The precipitation commenced with a drizzle, but the clouds suddenly released their heavy loads. Torrential showers began pouring down on The Common like sheets, as if descending from a pent-up waterfall.

James quickly ran out of the park through the deluge to hail an approaching taxi. He returned to his small, barely furnished flat, just north of the Charles River, on Alpine Street in Cambridge.

James had lived in Cambridge for roughly four years since he had been accepted to Harvard University, after his tenure as an honor student at Yale.

James Asher, Junior was born and raised in Connecticut, in the city of Hartford, where he lived with one of his aunts after his mother's death. His father, James Asher, Senior, was a prosperous banker employed by a large, established firm situated in downtown Boston and had its roots there for more than a century.

His father had died when James was only a child, and his mother had passed away during James' first year as a student at Yale. After the death of his mother, James inherited a considerable amount of capital—and he invested this money wisely.

James was always a hard-working and industrial-driven, resourceful individual. Although he was known for his asceticism and general self-discipline, James had two weaknesses. One was a lack of caution and prudence concerning important decisions. The other was his almost incessant habit of overworking.

As an undergraduate student, as in graduate school, James was known to study for hours, save for an occasional, casual break. Yet, in many ways, his mind was sharper than a diamond with a photographic memory, as he could recall almost everything he read verbatim after only one reading.

Now, in the comfort of his dry apartment, James took off his rain-soaked jacket and hung it in a closet.

The heavy rain continued to pour down unremittingly,

and its large, silvery beads pelted violently against the panes of James' flat. Drying his hair with a small towel, James went to his work desk and produced a large textbook, which he opened. The research for his dissertation was almost complete, and this particular volume was his last book to peruse prior to beginning his paper.

James was halfway through the text, yet he found it almost impossible to read or to comprehend in detail. This sudden lack of concentration was a recent development. James attempted to find the cause for the deficiency, yet he could come to no reasonable conclusion as to why he could no longer adequately study.

For the last two weeks, it seemed that James could not absorb the vital information in his texts wherever he was—whether in Boston, at Harvard Yard, in the libraries, cafes, or at The Common. As he sat now looking out at the rain, a thought suddenly dawned upon his psyche—perhaps what he needed most now was to get away from his familiar surroundings.   ✠

Chapter Two
The Cafe

The next afternoon was bright, refreshing, and sunny. James had just left his last class for the day, and decided to take a leisurely walk along the gleaming streets of Cambridge. Departing from the rectangular quad of Harvard Yard, he walked northeast, passing Sanders Theater Memorial Hall.

Today James felt confident, stepping on the sidewalks with a brisk, lively pace, stopping only once to light his pipe. Soon enough he found himself at the Juliet Café, just north of Washington Street. This particular cafe was popular with students and usually full of young people.

He took one of the white plastic chairs, choosing to dine indoors. Laying a menu on the table, a waitress duly introduced herself.

As James was reviewing the menu, his cell phone rang.

Removing the small phone from his coat pocket, he glanced at the device and saw a number he did not recognize. Nonetheless, he answered and heard a woman speak. From her manner, she was apparently a young woman.

"Hello, is this James Asher?"

Pausing momentarily, James answered, "Yes, this is James. May I ask who is calling?"

"My name is Susan, Susan Bennett. I am your cousin, James. I am calling from England. I have lived here in England all of my life."

Pausing again, James replied, "Then I assume we have never met since I have never been to England."

"No," the woman replied, "We have never met." Switching to a solemn tone, she continued, "That is why I am calling, James. I would very much like to meet you. I have heard so much about you; all of it has been good. I believe we have much in common and much to talk about.

"It is lovely here in the great mansion in the region of Basingstoke, Wiltshire. The name of the mansion is Wycliff Manor, and its extensive grounds are lovely. I am sure if you decide to make the journey, you will enjoy your stay immensely."

A pregnant and profound silence, in which neither spoke, ensued. James thought the phone call strange, incongruous as it was… and apropos of nothing, yet mysterious and intriguing.

To set at once upon a voyage to England was not a

commitment James could make in any immediate manner. Yet he did not wish to definitively close the door on the possibility. "I will think about it, Susan. Thank you for your kind invitation."

"I know what a hard-working student you are, James. Perhaps you would enjoy a leisurely sabbatical and might care to study in England, if only for a short time?"

Abruptly James asked Susan, "How are we related?"

"My mother was one of your many aunts who never left the British Isles."

James asked several more questions, including what Susan did for a living and whether she was married. She answered James' questions in detail and with alacrity. Yet when James asked for specific information regarding Wycliff Manor, Susan became suddenly vague.

James again thanked her, and the conversation ended.

For the next two weeks, James exerted himself in many futile attempts to manage any adVoncement in writing his dissertation. He simply could not write or even concentrate. No matter where James went in Boston, he could not make headway and he knew his Ph.D. depended on finishing it.

On a rainy Sunday afternoon, as James was pouring over notes written over a month ago, he watched the beads of rainwater travel lazily down his window. He was seated at his desk and mused upon the possibility of accepting his cousin's unorthodox invitation of staying in a far-off place—perhaps that might be the key to breaking his writer's block.

James thought, "Perhaps if I travel abroad, I might alleviate the attendant stress and whatever else might be preventing me from completing this all-important dissertation."

The following morning, along with his usual mail, James received a letter of foreign origin. The return address was marked Tilshead, Wiltshire, UK.

Opening the envelope, James saw a feminine script in an eloquent fashion.

Dear James,

I have known about you all of my life, ever since I was a girl. Your mother, Agnes, and my own were siblings. My mother never left England, and your mother never left the States after she emigrated to America from London as a girl.

However, I do know much about you. I know you and your mother lived north of Boston for most of the year, and you vacationed on Lake McDonough near Hartford, Connecticut, in southern New England in the summer months.

I know how you would recklessly climb boxwood trees near the lake until you came home with your knees badly cut and bruised.

I am familiar with how you would love to immerse yourself in the deep, green water of the lake when no one was watching and hold your breath far beneath its surface until everyone around you thought you were drowned.

I am aware that you are exceptionally bright, a Yale graduate with honors, and you acquired a scholarship to study at Harvard. I know you are a post-graduate student at Harvard now, where you study the humanities with a concentration in classical archeology.

I even know your favorite books and the authors who penned them: 'The Will to Power,' by Arthur Schopenhauer, Victor Hugo's 'Religious and Religion,' 'The Flowers of Evil,' by Charles Baudelaire, and Lord Byron's 'Don Juan.' And like Byron, I happen to know you share to this day a vitriolic hatred for the puritanical poetry of his contemporaries, Wordsworth and Coleridge. I am also conscious of how you frequently defy both time and space by flying off in your psyche to the ancient island of Lesbos to kneel at a shrine dedicated to Sappho and her pagan verse.

And I am deeply acquainted with the fact that you despise all religions, were always infatuated with Jean-Paul Sartre's private journals, and that his works 'The Age of Reason and Being and Nothingness' inspired your personal life philosophy. Understand, James, I am keenly aware that you believe humanity has no essence adjacent to its own existence because you are convinced that there is no God.

Furthermore, it is no secret to me that you keep your own autobiographical records in volumes similar to Sartre's.

These meticulous segments of information from James' formative and recent years were all true to fact. James was shocked and perplexed as to how Susan could possibly know of these facts relating to his past in such a precise and detailed manner. His hands began to shake as he continued reading the astonishing letter.

You must be wondering at this point in my correspondence how I am privy to such specific details about your life, James.

You see, I am a true clairvoyant and enjoy an adVonced state of extraordinary knowledge stemming from a lifelong involvement with various realms of the occult (if you happen to believe in such things). My uncle is well-informed in all matters of the occult, and I have learned much from him here at Wycliff.

I know your mother died when you were still a student at Yale. I am sorry that you lost her and that she passed so young. My mother is still living in England, despite her old age, in a suburb of Manchester.

I have been living for many years at the castle with my uncle. There are over one hundred rooms here at Wycliff Manor, and you are welcome to all of them. I am sure you would enjoy your stay here in the untamed woodlands near Tilshead, should you decide to make the trip over the Atlantic.

I have heard so much about you and I would absolutely love to meet you.

The Manor and its grounds have been here since the height of the fourteenth century. All was built upon a massive hill encompassing an enormous amount of land, roughly 4,000 acres. Its boundaries enclose cloisters, gardens, courtyards, and two ancient graveyards. All of these features were added to the grounds shortly after the completion of the house.

It is lovely here in the midst of the woodlands, and I know you would be very happy if you were to come to the wilds of the Salisbury Plain. You would find it pleasantly peaceful and could work on your studies undisturbed. I am in high hopes that you will make the effort to come to the Manor to enjoy its lovely and historic surroundings.

Should you decide to travel to my country, after you arrive in London, you will have to travel by train from Liverpool Station to the County of Wiltshire, southwest of the capital city. Once reaching the district of Wiltshire, you will continue to travel southward to Salisbury and then go by bus to the small, rustic old village of Tilshead, the closest town to the Manor itself.

When you arrive in the village, you will notice, at the end of the main road which goes through the town, an inn on the southwestern edge of the village. The name of the inn is Tilshead Lodge.

You will notice the Lodge without difficulty as a large, hanging wooden sign is displayed with the words Tilshead Lodge engraved upon it above the front porch. There, you will also find several old wooden benches below the porch's awning.

Wycliff Manor is about four kilometers (or roughly two and a half miles) west of the Lodge, at the far end of a dense forest. There is a fairly well-beaten horse trail you can navigate without much difficulty. I will greet you at the entrance to the Manor, just beyond the main courtyard and cloister facing east at the front of the house.

Yours, with expectation,
Susan M. Bennet   ♱

Chapter Three
On Leaving Boston

After three more grueling days of incessant writer's block, James Asher, Junior finally decided to accept his cousin's invitation to venture off to the south of England. Soon after James made this decision, he realized he should learn all he could relating to Wycliff Manor and the region where he was bound.

In Susan's letter, she noted that Wycliff Manor was an ancient and historic mansion located at the end of an apparently uninhabited forest near the town of Tilshead. She had also written that the Manor dated back to the middle part of the fourteenth century.

In his extensive reading that day, James found a detailed account of the region, and it was fascinating.

The village of Tilshead is close to the geographical center of Salisbury Plain, on the A360 road, approximately forty-eight miles southwest of London, near the River Till's source.

James read on:

In the high Middle Ages, Tilshead played host to various Kings of England as they traveled throughout their realms creating a healthy local economy. At the time of Domesday, Tilshead belonged to King Edward III and had to render one night's lodging each year for him and his household. By the arrival of the middle part of the fourteenth century, the tithing (or administrative center of Tilshead) was an expansive abbey named Wycliff Manor, an enormous, castellated mansion. Its construction had commenced in 1326 and was completed in 1334.

The mansion still exists to this day and is situated in a detached part of forestland outside the boundaries of the town.

Wycliff Manor's construction was overseen by King Edward III (also known as Edward of Windsor) prior to his rise to the throne.

King Edward III transformed the Kingdom of England into one of Northern Europe's most formidable military powers. His fifty-year reign was one of the most brutal in medieval history, yet he saw vital reforms in law and government. Edward was crowned at the age of fourteen after his father was deposed by his mother, Isabella of France. Two years later, the crown went to her lover, Roger Mortimer.

At the age of seventeen, Edward III led a successful coup against Roger Mortimer, whom Edward killed by nailing Mortimer to a wall. And so began the despotic, tyrannical reign of King Edward III.

Thus ended the article on the history of the area. As for Wycliff Manor, James could find no further details.

Nothing else about the Manor was noted in any of the other books he was able to obtain.

The following morning, Saturday, May 7, James left early for Boston's Logan Airport in Winthrop. He procured a ticket for a six-hour and thirty-minute flight with American Airlines to London's Heathrow International Airport. The ticket was for Tuesday morning, May 10—a few days' time.

James estimated his arrival at the mansion would take place on May 10, or more likely, the following day, the day of his expected arrival.

That Tuesday, James arrived by cab at Boston's Logan Airport by 8:00 AM. It was a bright and sunny spring day on the East Coast. His flight was due to depart for London at 9:00 that morning. James tended to walk briskly and with a youthful stride. This morning was no different as he made his way to the airline terminal.

Sitting uncomfortably on a small, round chair in a bar close to the terminal's exit, James ordered a glass of beer. Reaching into the right pocket of his peacoat, he pulled out Susan's letter and reread it. When he was done, he placed the letter back into his coat pocket and ordered another bottle of dark brown Belgian ale.

At a quarter to 9:00, James heard over the intercom that his plane was preparing for departure. He arose from his stool, placed two twenty dollar bills on the wooden table before him, and left the bar. Walking slowly through the terminal annex, up through an open aired conveyance stairway, James proceeded to board the plane. He felt more than a little nervous as he produced his ticket and found his way to his designated seat.

James was not nearly himself. He was going to a faraway country to be among people he had never met. His seat was in the rear right corner of first class, next to an oval window and James promptly closed the shade as soon as he sat down. As the jet commenced to taxi down the wide runway, the plan suddenly attained a great speed and ascended powerfully off the ground.

After a few minutes of rapid ascent, the huge airline leveled off and reached its standard flying height over the Atlantic Ocean. James reclined in his comfortable chair and eventually fell asleep.

In three hours' time, the plane was hovering over the abyss of the boundless sea when it encountered a violent storm. The great jet shook in the sudden and violent tempest. James awoke, shaken in his seat, his head thrown liberally back and forth by the violent turbulence. He raised the window shade and was shocked to see nothing but a billowy, dim, and dangerous brine of black, rolling clouds. The clouds encompassed the entirety of the aircraft, pressing against every visible prism of the cabin's many tiny windows.

James heard himself moan as he felt the seat belt tightly squeeze his waist. It continued from the force of the gigantic plane's erratic, jolted movements. As James continued looking out his window, he could perceive nothing but the most violent aspects of nature's fury.

A wild torrent of rain began to beat against the sides

and roof of the aircraft mercilessly. The dynamic attack of wild water pelted the plane with a menacing force. A bolt of lightning almost struck the plane, just barely missing a wing.

The faces of the other passengers betrayed the varied sensations of utter panic. As the wild plane shook madly, rolling left and right, a chorus of screams rumbled through the cabin.

The stewards ceased to serve or tend the passengers— or even walk down the carpeted aisle; in fear, they all retreated to the rear of the plane to buckle down. Glossy red "Please Put On Seat Belt" signs were flashing alarmingly.

Then, the sky rapidly abruptly cleared as if by an occult force or by the eerie hand of some curious brand of magic. Within the space of a few short moments, the entire atmosphere above, below, and around the plane became quiet; the clouds dissipated, the sun reemerged, and all appeared perfectly calm once more.

James and his fellow passengers heard the captain announce, "All Clear" over the intercom after making a brief and bewildering apology.

About three hours later, the vast plane flew smoothly for the remainder of the flight until it landed on schedule at London's Heathrow Airport. James grabbed his satchel in hand, exited the plane, and soon walked onto London streets beneath a dark, overcast sky.

He hailed a small, green taxi on this foggy English night. It was late in the evening over the mighty metropolis. James took the swiftly driven cab to Liverpool Station and boarded a modern-looking train southbound for the region of Salisbury.

When the train arrived at Salisbury station, the time was close to midnight. James realized he must wait until the next morning before boarding the bus bound for the small village of Tilshead.

As many tourists among him were journeying on to see the sights of Stonehenge. James registered at a modern Hilton in the center of town to stay in one of its fine rooms. As the night sky was brightly lit with stars and a full moon, James decided to see what he could of the immediate area before retiring.

Roaming the streets, he found a delightfully manicured field to walk through and came upon Queen Elizabeth Gardens.

In the distance, James could see the lovely banks of a glistening river. A provincial, old sign was posted next to a dreamy willow tree on which was written "The River Avon." As it diverted through the gardens, the river was framed by colorful throngs of beautiful flora which glittered in the moonlight.

The water ran calmly, flowing broadly into a rippling lake from a clear, wide stream. As James sat on a patch of tall, holly-hued grass at one of its banks, a strange older man approached, half crippled and poorly clothed.

Gazing momentarily into James' eyes, the stranger asked him where he was going.

"Wycliff Manor," James replied.

As soon as James answered, the elderly gentleman warned, "You do not know where you are going, young man. If you knew what awaits you in that place, you would go no further. And if you go there, you will wish you had never come to such a house."

James retorted: "What is your reason for such a warning?"

The mysterious gentleman replied in a loud and imperious voice which seemed to sail over the entire lake, "Save yourself, young man! Leave and go back home, wherever you came from!"

The stranger walked away without speaking another word, his cane in hand, until he was no longer in sight.   ✟

Chapter Four
The Lodge

James awoke very late in his hotel room the next
morning, as the bus leaving for Tilshead was not
scheduled to depart until 4:00 in the afternoon. He called
for room service to request a late lunch. Fifteen minutes
later, a young female serVont entered James' room with a
tray of food.

After enjoying the meal beside his bed, James
passed his remaining time at Salisbury Station, smoking
his pipe and reading a brochure on the history of the
region. At fifteen minutes to 4:00, the bus for Tilshead
arrived. James surveyed the vehicle and secured a seat for
himself toward the back. The bus was mostly vacant
save for a few elderly locals. As the conveyance journeyed
slowly southwest, an all-encompassing gloomy fog
arose from the surface of the road on which the bus was
traveling. James abruptly fell asleep in preparation for the
short, rural stretch of travel left to him.

As his casual sleep progressed, James felt his psyche

descend into a dark and heavy slumber. In the space of minutes, his unconscious state became even deeper, and he began to see clearly in his mind a castle-like mansion lit by a flaming moon perched high upon a massive hill. In one of its tall, arched windows, a dark, mystical light glowed from within the tallest tower.

And through that cryptic opening,
a ghostly, demonic face gazed down through the
long, parted drapes of the stone encased glass—
but spoke not a word.

At that moment, the front wheels of the bus ran into a shallow ditch. James awoke from his dreadful dream in a fearful state from the sudden shaking. Looking out the window, he could see imposing collages of swampy, foggy, reed-covered moors. The more elevated of these moors generally looked dryer but no less ominous.

About a mile down the road, as the bus entered the town of Tilshead, James thought he had never in his life beheld such a place of eerie desolation. The few bare trees lining the main road were foreboding, and the air was heavy, stagnant, and foul-smelling. A few beggars were clamoring by the site of the road. The bus drew to a still as rain immediately began coming down heavily.

James took his lone carry-on bag in hand and descended from the bus. He was immediately soaked in the deluge. He desperately looked for the refuge of the lodge his cousin had written he would find at the far end of town. After a long walk passing vacant houses and several dilapidated shops with broken windows, James found Tilshead Lodge. It was just as it was described in his cousin's letter.

The lodge was completely rustic in appearance, with a few beech trees standing out front. A few worn oak benches stood in a row underneath the time-weathered awning. Behind the row of benches stood two large, dusty windows with the main entryway of the lodge sandwiched between them.

The main entry consisted of two wooden doors framing the main entrance. Strangely enough, as soon as James walked under the porch awning, the heavy rain suddenly and completely ceased.

He walked coolly and casually into the lodge and beheld several people to the left sitting in old booths made of pinewood aside a paneled, wooden barricade. Most patrons ceased eating and drinking to look keenly at the conspicuous stranger who was suddenly in their midst.

To James' right, he found a timbered bar of antiquated pine. Two coats of arms hung from a palisade between two sections of the inn; beyond was another dining room, complete with more old-fashioned booths where a few more people were seated. James surveyed the local patrons for a few moments as they stared at him in a curious manner. Calmly, he looked away and sat at the bar.

Behind the bar stood a heavily built older man wearing a large, brown hat. This man and his wife,

Elizabeth, owned the lodge. The man was its primary barkeep. As James attempted to get more comfortable in his seat, the innkeeper touched the rim of his hat and said in a welcoming manner, "Good day, Sir. Welcome to Tilshead Lodge."

James tersely replied, "Good day."

The old man held a shiny, silver decanter, "Care for a glass of wine, Sir?"

James appreciated the offer but asked, "Might I have a brandy, please?"

"Certainly, Sir," the innkeeper replied. "We have the best brandy in all of England here." Returning with a bottle of fine brandy, the barkeep asked, "Traveling far, young man?"

"Not much farther, I hope… Would it be possible for me to have a meal?"

"Well, yes, Sir. But only a simple one, I am afraid."

The innkeeper turned to a buxom middle-aged woman wearing a broad, white apron standing at the bar's far end. "Do go and fetch this gentleman a meal, please, Elizabeth." Turning back to James, he explained, "We don't get many wayfarers in these parts."

"I would not know," replied James. "I am traveling westward."

"Westward? Why there's nothing west of this town but brushwood and forestland," the innkeeper exclaimed. "Where are you off to? For I've never seen your face here before, and I know every soul who comes here to

Tilshead Lodge. And what is more, they all know me. But, from your mannerisms and your way of speaking, my guess is you're a stranger in these parts."

"Yes, indeed, I am a stranger here; I am not even from your country. I have come here to Tilshead from the United States. I have ventured all the way from my home in Boston. My destination is here in Wiltshire to a house called Wycliff Manor, a huge and ancient house — I trust you know the place? I understand it is close to these grounds, in this vicinity. Perhaps you know it well? Perhaps you are acquainted with the mansion?"

At these last inquisitions, the chaperon's face turned pale and drawn with fear, and his head abruptly looked down at the wooden slab of the bar. His countenance continued to manifest a disturbed and alarmed expression. He walked away without saying another word.

While the barkeep retreated to one of the back rooms, his wife Elizabeth returned with a simple meal consisting of potatoes, carrots, and unseasoned beef wreathed with a strand of some sort of celery. The dish was presented on a gleaming silver tray.

Laying the food on the bar in front of James, Elizabeth saw the enigmatic look in James' inscrutable expression, devoid of any utterance. She found it necessary to explain her husband's strange silence regarding James' questions pertaining to the mysterious mansion ostensibly located at the far end of the forestland west of the lodge.

"You must understand, my good, young man; we

hardly see new faces enter Tilshead Lodge, and the new faces we do see know better than to go in that direction."

James felt a compunction to ask a simple and direct question, "But why? Why does the very name of this place produce nothing but expressions of fearful loathing and deliberate attempts to evade any general discussion regarding the place?"

Listening to the voices of the customers and hearing that all of them had returned their focus to their private dinner conversations, Elizabeth answered James' questions with one sentence, albeit in a very low whisper.

"Because, my young friend, the place is haunted."

James quickly retorted, "And how in heaven's name do you know that?" He found the barkeeper's wife's answer to be unsettling, to say the least.

"Because once, when I was only ten, my grandfather took me fishing near the mansion. He told me he needed some live bait and walked behind the castle where the soil was moist.

"A large, ancient cemetery was situated behind the house, and a thick, dank mist covered the graveyard. Believing my eyes were deceiving me, I saw two hands in the fog over an open grave grab, in a state of fury, onto what looked like the bough of an oak tree."

James asked, "They were obviously your grandfather's hands, then, correct?"

Making sure her husband was not near, Elizabeth continued hovering over the bar to whisper into James' ear, "I wish with all my heart that I could say the words you have just uttered were the truth. But my good man — just then, the fog cleared, and what I thought was a bough was my grandfather's leg, and I witnessed the body and soul of my grandfather being taken down alive into the jaws of that abysmal grave.

"And lo and behold, those hands, those hands, those awful hands—were not of this earth."

As she completed her story, the barkeeper emerged from the kitchen to politely ask James, with a noticeable degree of apprehension, "Is everything to your liking, Sir?"

Without her husband seeing, Elizabeth placed her forefinger over her mouth, warning James to keep his silence about what she had just confided.

Without looking directly at either person, James replied, "Yes, thank you, the food is fine and more than adequate."

James abruptly finished the remainder of his meal. As the barkeep's wife carried away his tray, the innkeeper noticed a disturbed look on James' face.

"Wouldn't you rather prefer to remain at the lodge for the night instead of going any further west? Perhaps you'll reconsider pursuing your voyage further into the woods? We have several fine cabins here on the second floor."

"Thank you for your kind invitation, Sir," replied James, "but I am expected at the manor, and I must complete my quest. Do you know any more details regarding the mansion before I embark on the final stretch of my undertaking?"

In a dark and somber tone, the innkeeper replied, "Look, Sir. You're a stranger here in Tilshead. Some things are best left as they are and not to be bothered with. You ordered a meal, Sir. As the owner of this lodge, it's my duty to serve you. Now that you've eaten it, I ask that you go and leave us here in peace."

The owner could see a look of consternation and perplexity on James' face, and then with all the grave tenses of a dim and dusky, chilling inflection, he asked:

"Do you know where you are going?

And among what sort of people?

Do you know what kinds of things you are going to?"

Retaining his reticence, James was becoming disturbed and annoyed at what was apparently the survival of a foolish hybrid of medieval folklore, of strange old legends and regional superstitions.

Seeing the determination in James' eyes, the innkeeper said, "I suppose you daft Yanks do whatever you wish whenever you set up your heads up to do them. I know you see things in a very different kind of light than we plain folks do here in the shadows of the moors. But this is Tilshead Village, my friend. It is a world away from the garish glow of London—and a universe away from all of those showy lights there in your New York City. You Yanks weren't very welcome here in the war against Hitler, and you're even less welcome here now."

James quietly reached into his coat pocket and laid twenty-five pounds on the bar. Earlier, on his way into the inn, as James looked beyond the rear dining room through a large, dusty window, he had noticed an old, worn-down barn and a very unkempt-looking horse stable adjacent to the rear of the lodge. He asked the owner, "May I hire a horse for the remainder of my excursion?"

Between several satisfied smiles, the owner answered, "We just lost two mares, and the one living gelding bred to hire is too ill to travel. I'm sorry, Sir. You will have to make the journey on foot."

James placed another twenty pounds into the hands of the owner.

"Well, Sir, if you insist on finding the manor by sundown, you'll have to walk through a long, dark forest, and you've roughly an hour left of daylight, at most.

Only one old path leads from this lodge to the vicinity of the manor. The trail is quite obscure at points, as many overgrown grasses make it hard to navigate through the woods without getting lost. The mansion is roughly four kilometers from here."

James gave the innkeeper another ten pounds, so the owner went on.

"Although the trail is thin and obscure at points, you should be able to avoid getting lost if you depart straight away while the sun is still upon you. You'll need an accurate compass to work with… If you hurry, you should reach the manor in about an hour."

With that, the curator of the inn tipped his hat, and James acquiesced with a courtly bow. James then turned his head to gaze upon the start of the forest and nodded back to the owner with a hint of genuine gratitude. Looking westward at the edge of the coppice, James departed taking out his compass.

As he walked on the grassy floor into the shaded woods, he did so with a sense of trepidation. And as he made his slow progress into the woods, James thought, "The regional superstitions of the villagers are more than formidable, this being the year 2021. A potent belief in the occult and other superstitious ways have well exceeded any righteous reason in the minds of the ignorant town dwellers."

Such were James' thoughts, which he soon forgot all about as he realized the sun was commencing to descend. He had to hurry for the mansion lest he should get lost in the dense old forest in the darkness of the night.

Twenty minutes after leaving the inn, James found himself amid a thick, pilous forest. For the remainder of his pilgrimage, James walked through the orange-colored woodland, the sun bleeding hazily through many leaf-clad boughs.

As he journeyed westward at a steady pace, James noticed songbirds were singing less and less on the tips of the branches. As the sun was slowly setting over the tree-laden glades, the last rays of daylight began to throw long, slender silhouettes on the green and yellow grasses.

James walked on beneath hovering branches, up and down sloping fields, over streams and rivulets. As he ventured deeper into the woodland, it was as if a medieval spirit had descended from the sky and taken its hold over the entire land, for the atmosphere was changing. It seemed to James as though he was leaving the modern world. The birds ceased singing altogether. The moon began to show itself high above the tips of the forest. As James was crossing one stream in particular, which was wider than previous streams, he noticed several unique characteristics.

Until now, the streams and rivulets had been calm and docile, tame in size and flow of their currents. Yet, the current in this stream was violent, gushing forward with froth as it rushed rolling southward. Crests on the wild surface of this brook were white-tipped and toppled over its various large, flat stones with a rigorous rapidity.

This waterway seemed to mark a boundary between two distinct atmospheres. The prior atmosphere appeared to be relatively tame, somewhat docile, and even serene, yet the air on the other side of the stream seemed ancient, thunderous, and ominous.

James maneuvered his way across the stream by making use of the more elevated stones peaking just above the level of the furious current. The time seemed short when James ascertained the other side of the spouting trough.

As he regained his composure standing in the tall, dry grass, James felt he had suddenly entered a bygone era, where the modernity of the twenty-first century ceased to exist, and monarchs of the past rose from their crypts. From those dusty, old history books James had read and knew only too well, it seemed that those long-dead figures had come to life. And although he witnessed no specter in his psyche nor his senses, as he continued on his way, James felt the long, regal dead had somehow reincarnated into a lively, new, and strange reality of the living. ✞

Chapter Five
The Manor

As James approached Wycliff Manor, he could feel a new and disturbing vibration from an otherworldly aura. This sensation was extenuated by the fact that now, the sunlight had faded completely, and a thick, nebulous darkness had taken its prominence over the starless fields of the forested glades. Most strange to James was that although it was May, the air was decisively colder, as though James had left a docile atmosphere and entered an inclement and hostile weather zone. Time seemed endless as James walked onward through the reedy remainder of the gloomy forest.

Finally, a clearing arose before him, and immediately beyond it rose a grassy, steep, and expansive hill. James could see a long, wide stairway of worn, ancient stone leading up the mount at a gradual angle of ascent. His boots rang out loudly as they scraped the stone of the moss-covered walkway.

All at once, the stone-paved steps merged into a level plain that opened onto a vast and dilapidated courtyard, immediately beyond which James could see the immense and ancient edifice of Wycliff Manor.

On the other side of this courtyard sat two vast symmetrical sections of the mansion jettisoning outward to frame the entire square. High above these partitions, two of the manor's four bell towers were just barely visible from the courtyard.

As he crossed the large, dark courtyard's chipped marble floor through several tall, broad, and eerie silhouettes, he passed several dead fountains and gray, flaking, ancient statues. At last, he arrived at the manor's main entrance.

An old, iron door marked the entry, on which hung a rusty metal knocker molded in the form of a lion's head. As there were no doorbells, James employed the knocker three times as loud as he could.

A dark and foul-smelling pond not far from the cloistered entrance permeated the area with a miasmic vapor. The entire edifice and grounds surrounding Wycliff Manor appeared cursed by a solemn condemnation. A bitter, chilling breeze threw dead leaves around James' boots.

After waiting in the cold night air for nearly twenty minutes, James knocked twice more; still no response. He was beginning to wonder if the immense house was unoccupied. Aside from two antique lanterns dimly lit on either side of the doorway, James could see no other lights stemming from the manor's many tall windows.

Just as James was considering leaving the huge, foreboding house and commencing the long walk back to the village, he noticed the great old portal slowly opening from the inside. The creaking ancient door left a wide gap in the threshold, revealing a tall, distinguished-looking older man wearing a white shirt with ruffled sleeves. He peered into James' eyes for a moment and calmly introduced himself in a voice that carried out into the courtyard with an odd sort of ring that echoed for many meters around the enclosed vestibule.

"I am Baron William Charles Von Drake, and you must be the young Master James Asher, Junior from America. Welcome to Wycliff Manor."

The baron paused momentarily and smiled grimly, "I assume you were expecting your cousin Susan to greet you. Regrettably, Susan is tending, nursing, what you will, her sick, elderly mother and is currently away. But the night winds are cold, and you must be tired and hungry after your long journey. Let me see to your comfort myself. Please, do come in."

James considered the baron's greeting warm and cordial enough to accept. James slowly took two steps forward with uneasiness and caution stepping into the manor's prodigious main foyer. Stately marble busts were seated on ivory pedestals situated on either side of the great hall.

The baron led James up a wide, circular stairway to the second floor and down a long, dimly lit corridor graced with regal-looking portraits. James recognized a few portraits depicting English kings from the middle ages. At the end of the corridor, one such portrait was especially known to James as that of King Edward III, otherwise known as "The Black Prince." ♰

Chapter Six
The Fireplace

Having reached the end of the hall, the baron led James up an ancient stone staircase and down another long hallway. Opening a door to the right, the baron led James into a medium-sized chamber, facing the west, which was to be James' bed chamber.

This room featured in its far left corner, against a wall, an old Victorian-styled bed with long, off-white drapes hanging on all sides, kept in place by four tall wooden legs made of fine oak. To the immediate right of the bed between two high slender windows was a large writing desk with draws fashioned in its lower shelves.

Both windows looked out the western portion of the estate far below upon a graveyard. Overall, the bed chamber gave off an austere and grim appearance. As James removed the satchel he was wearing over his right shoulder and placed it on the bed, the baron spoke:

"This shall be your private chamber, my friend. And you may use any of the rooms on this floor for your purposes. Now, let us sojourn to the dining room below. I am sure you must be very hungry." The two men then retraced their steps down the halls and stairway until the baron turned the handle of an old oak door.

Within, James beheld a mammoth and stately chamber. On the far side of the large room, thin embers of a dying fire rose listlessly from a rock-sheathed hearth up a wide, brick chimney. Brightly colored, emblematic flags hung from casements on either side of the huge fireplace. Opposite the grate, on the other side of the room, stood a half-furnished dining table with freshly prepared food.

The baron walked toward a tall, stone-encased window. After a long pause, he stood completely still and laid his hand upon a grand marble mantelpiece. In a reverent tone, he began to speak. His deep, imperious voice rang out among the corners of the monumental chamber.

"What you see here my young friend, are the remnants of a noble house, ghosts, relics of past victories in bygone times of excessive bloodshed, political treachery, and war. And yet, I am proud of my noble heritage in these times of false and ignoble peace, borne alone from pathetic cowardice and a collective spiritual malaise among men and nations alike.

"I am descended from a mighty Saxon people and a

truly great monarch who avenged his father's murder with one swift and merciless blow. And when that opportunity presented itself, he brooked no hesitation. The peasantry called him "The Black Prince." Yet what do peasants know?

"Aside from placing brick upon brick, what is their purpose devoid of a King to rule them? Without no head to rule their inferior members, they would not even know where to place the cornerstone in the rising of a common chapel or a simple house. All peasants drift into idleness without a King to rule and guide them."

As he continued, the baron became excited, grasping ever tighter the tier of the alabaster mantelpiece.

"Indeed, the wise and magnanimous brain of a wealthy and truly great monarch and the poor hands of simple peasants built this once noble and glorious manor. True, some of the grandeur of this house has faded. Yet its many halls and chambers still represent a ruthless and righteous regal power."

When the baron ceased to speak, he motioned James to the dining table with a courteous wave of his hand. As James sat down, the baron stepped over to a large, elaborate cabinet covered by two golden veils. As he parted the gilded curtains, there, in the recess, were many fine exquisite liquors housed in splendid decanters sitting upon several wide wooden shelves.

After James took his seat at the table, the baron asked, "Would you care for some cognac?"

Feigning a coolness of emotional composure that he

did not possess, James replied, "Yes, please, Baron, indeed, I am partial to cognac."

The baron smiled as he poured the spirit into James' flask. The cognac was of the finest genuine Napoleonic Brandy. James found it more than excellent to his taste and said so.

"Please, do eat as you wish," instructed the baron.

James began to consume the large plate of food laid before him, consisting of an excellent and generous helping of well-cooked pork, a salad, and a large plate of buttered potatoes. Of the brandy, James had two glasses. As James ate, Baron Von Drake sat on the opposite side of the long pine table watching James with a curious interest.

James ate his supper with moderate relish in the presence of his imposing host. As James placed his fork upon the table to lift his glass, the baron reclined in his ornate chair studded with the finest gems.

"I have never been outside of Europe. Yet, I have always respected the 'great colonies of King George III.'" the baron explained.

James understood the baron was referring to the United States, a Country with many liberal freedoms the baron had long despised. The baron then began to ask James many questions regarding "the colonies," as the baron called them. He was especially eager to learn more about America's long-surviving government as a Constitutional Republic—and he especially wanted to hear how it achieved its fierce, global military dominance.

James finished his drink and softly placed the chalice in his right hand on the table with as much composure as he could feign. He thought for a moment— and then, to please his host, James answered the baron's questions with as much insight as he could articulate.

"I believe the enormous resources of my country, coupled with its industry, led to its current military dominance. Vast and varied resources and industry enabled the United States to enjoy its current worldwide projectile powers." James concluded, "It is my assertion, baron, that America gained these adVontages over decades of technological adVoncements in the various empirical sciences."

"Ah!" exclaimed the baron. "Excellent! For what virtue can any nation possess devoid of the iron hammer of an utterly brutal army of force?"

As the two men spoke, James felt the baron possessed a dark, ethereal quality about him; he seemed to radiate a fearful aura of some intangible yet potent malevolence of spirit. James' conviction was that this evil reigned deep, even into the very core of the mighty old mysterion's heart—nothing but the purest evil existed there.

The baron had never been seen in Tilshead—as he had never ventured forth from the boundaries of the immense old house. On one point, James could harbor no illusions. The haunting sense of a moral deformity with which the nobleman had mastered and impressed upon all his beholders was authentic.

Upon this last consideration, James Asher, Junior could not but experience a frightful shiver in the whole of his body, which do as he may, he could not conceal.

As James glanced at the pale and pallid features of the baron, the baron, observing the disturbed look on James' face asked, "Is anything amiss, Master James?"

James made a fitful and stuttering reply, "No, Baron Von Drake, nothing is amiss. And the meal was more than splendid, thank you."

The baron produced a diabolic smile which would make Pilate envious and said, "You must understand, my young American friend, this great ancient house can play tricks on your mind. And if you are not too careful in exercising the virtue of prudence, coupled with the use of the right reason, your very sanity might betray you.

"It has happened here before, at Wycliff Manor, long ago from the very days of the construction of this house. Aside from your cousin Susan, you and I are its only occupants. This old house has seen a great many years. The last young man who stayed here met with an untimely death one freezing January morning—by hanging himself, no less. His name was Sir John Kenneth Dwight, if I remember correctly; he was a painter of sorts. At least he used to be."

Most disturbing to James was the fact that the baron's physical appearance bore a striking resemblance to the tall, broad portrait of King Edward III, which James had taken keen notice of in the outer hallway. James languidly arose from the old pine table and asked the baron to show him back to his room.

Before they could begin to leave, the moonlight which had permeated the entire cabin all the while suddenly seemed to vacillate in a wild manner commencing to illuminate one distinct corner of the chamber. A haunted-looking nook was situated to the left of the fireplace. The dying embers in the grate at once revived into livid flames which began to throw godless, gleaming rivers of unholy light upon the vast marble floor. And as these wild flames grew ever more fierce, rising higher into the air, slender silhouettes appeared to exceed the limits of the immense chamber until an all-pervasive darkness rose and deepened wherever the long brooks of fire did not prevail. It seemed to James that the fury of the scarlet blaze was summoned from the nethermost region of hell itself.

To his amazement, James perceived something white emerging from the moonlit corner. The baron beheld the rising fire and mysterious specimen cryptically emerging from the blackness of the nook with a blissful demonic smile.

To James' horror, he could see that the white being approaching him was, in fact, an animated skeleton. Its ivory-hued bones were half-clothed with putrid flesh. As it opened its mouth attempting to speak, the bottom of its pearly jaw simply fell agape in silence. James' face turned wan and pallid before he ran out of the chamber into the hallway as the monster hopelessly screamed as if it were among the damned, its bones forever condemned to the fury of the unhallowed flames.

When James finally ascertained the quiet of his room, he slammed the door shut on the baron. Not having a key, in an abject state of panic, he dragged a huge Vonity chest that lay beneath one of the two windows and placed it against the door should the thing attempt to break in.

One thing was now certain. Any illusions James had initially harbored that Wycliff Manor was an innocuous place where he could work on his paper in a leisurely environment were now entirely shattered.   ✟

Chapter Seven
The Attic

Other places in England, especially in May, radiated a cheerful, and in some regions, even a sunny glow. Yet the usual atmosphere surrounding Wycliff Manor exuded only dreary, dark, and soundless days.

The following morning James awoke early. His sleep had been tortured with vivid nightmares of virulent dead, malicious spirits, and other malevolent entities of varied kinds. James now had but one singular and overriding concern—escaping the manor and everything around it as soon as he possibly could. He spent the majority of the day in his room looking over a detailed map of Wiltshire which he had acquired from the lodge.

Although the exact location of the manor was not listed on the chart, James could decipher other details including approximately where he was and the best and most efficient means out of the region and to safety. He decided to escape from the mansion to the north, as there might be another town nearby since that portion of the land was not featured on the map. Later that afternoon, a curtain of eerie gray billows hovered oppressively low over the entirety of the mansion and its melancholy grounds.

On one side of the manor, not far from the house in the northern woods, beneath the bare arched boughs of shadowy trees, lay a still, small, and nebulous pond. And despite the frequent visitations of rustling winds, the whole pool was perpetually devoid of ripples on its gloomy surface. These desolate breezes, which covered the entirety of the area, violently shook the tall, dead reeds lining the little lake, yet the water remained unmoved.

As the afternoon sunlight became further obscured by the amassing vapor of menacing clouds, James found himself roving amid the mist of the northern woods. All around him, the air was permeated with a loathsome silence as James wandered further north in mysterious shadows of long and dour silhouettes.

As he continued to venture deeper into the woods, over tall, slender-leaved plants and sunless rivulets, James came upon the reedy border of the ominous-looking pond. Although he stood on the edge of the bog, he could not see the extent of the marshland's depth since the watery morass was heavily clouded.

As James stood placidly looking into the vacant well on

a sallow patch of grass at the water's edge, the saturnine figure of a dead man began to emerge from its sodden grave.

Gazing wildly up at James, the anguished being exclaimed in a state of extreme despondency, "Does your soul still harbor life within? Heed my words! I live beyond the grace of God! Take me from the endless lament of this tearful tomb!"

Suddenly a throng of demons, like sentinels from hell, descended from the tawdry sky and perched themselves on the many boughs which covered the pond and its every border. James looked on in terror as the corpse grasped the edge of a large stone on one of the banks of the basin with both hands. He was attempting to extract himself from the lurid pool using all the strength within his being.

As the demons above him began to laugh, another damned soul wrapped his baneful hands around the former's ankles from behind. In the following instant, the morbid corpse attempting to escape let out an appalling and monstrous scream as he was swiftly and forcefully pulled backward into the murky water, never to be seen again.

James fled from the lake at a great speed ascertaining the main foyer of the mansion. Upon doing so, he searched the immediate vicinity for some kind of weapon in case he might have to defend himself, but he failed to find anything adequate.

As the night descended over Wiltshire, bringing

a lively wind with a shrouded moon obscured by more grim clouds, James noticed three strange items of interest within the vast mansion.

The first oddity was when James awoke earlier that morning and discovered his cell phone missing from his coat. He thought that, perhaps, he had misplaced the device behind the Vonity table. Yet after doing some meticulous detective work, James found his phone was not only missing from the floor behind the Vonity—it was missing from the entire room. Another other oddity James had by now come into contact with was despite the evident wealth of the estate, the mansion housed no servants. In addition, candles, not electricity, were employed to light the mansion's countless halls and chambers.

Sitting on his bed, James paused to listen to determine if any noises were coming from the recesses, corridors, or the manor's towers. After hearing nothing, he decided to venture without to see which would be the fastest route to escape when the opportunity arose—should the main door be locked. James briskly flew down two stories to the main floor and out to Wycliff Manor's eastern courtyard.

The sky featured a thick steely throng of horizontal clouds. The evening air, being closed in and close to the ground as it was, betrayed a foul-smelling miasma that James found repulsive to his soul. The entire night was anathema to all the living but, perhaps, not to all the dead.

James now believed the entire estate of Wycliff Manor

did indeed house only the dead. He and the baron, he thought, were the only living beings within the entire place. James' one obsession now was to escape the mansion with all of the faculties of his reason still prudentially disposed and intact.

Oak trees hovered over the grounds like diabolic hands waiting to clutch any passersby and cast him into hell. Every dying, dim throng of myrtles and lindens appeared decisively haunted as they cryptically wavered. Their undulating boughs filled James with a profound sense of approaching and unavoidable danger. The sky was saturated with a gloom that seemed to manifest the darkest side of the afterlife in its opaque depths.

It seemed to James that in the distance, miles away, demonic phantoms were whispering in tongues in a far off farmhouse or perhaps in some abandoned cabin. He heard serpentine beings laughing in godless cottages to the east of the moors.

The pipes of the courtyard were leaking and rusted. The statues on the faded marble floor were ages old with peeling terra-cotta and strands of pale moss. One of these statues was of the Greek goddess Iris. It was a tall and forbidding artifact. James, an expert in Greek and English medieval art and archaeology, could see that the statue dated back to the fourteenth century. He also knew that in Greek mythology, Iris was the goddess of the rainbow and the primary messenger for other gods.

As James was studying the countenance of the stony figure, a black shadowy form arose behind it. The dark figure poured forth its energy into the form of the statute, which became animated in an incredible manner. The entire countenance of the statue transformed from a pale, lifeless grayish-white color to a gleaming, lively, animated red.

To James' disbelief, the eyes of the frozen figure ceased to stupidly gaze at the sky and turned their terrible gaze straight into James' own. Its mouth moved and the image spoke.

"You resemble the One I despise—for you are a man, made in His image, the image of my immortal enemy. Begone!" The statue smiled a most hellish grin as a frothy stream of blood gushed from its gaping mouth.

James fell into a paralysis of fear. High above his head he heard the sound of clanging metal, as if someone or something were banging a pipe with a metallic instrument. The sound seemed to come from the highest pinnacles of the manor, somewhere among the four towers.

Each tower marked a corner of the chateau, indicating with exactitude the four points of the compass. These round, stony spires of Wycliff Manor exceeded twenty-five feet in height from the base of the castle's roof.

James thought the clanging noises were perhaps fashioned by the hand of someone in distress calling for help. The red, demonic figure behind the statue was now gazing at the sky. Suddenly, the demon beheld a holy being and fled into the chateau by passing through a wall. The horrid statue ceased bleeding, and its eyes returned to a dead, stony gray once more. James could hardly believe what he just witnessed.

Without hesitation, he left the marble patio and ran into the eastern foyer, up the circular staircase to the second floor. As the clanging became decisively louder, James was convinced the noise emanated from one of the towers above him.

At the end of a long narrow corridor, James saw the entrance to a narrow stone stairway opposite the main dining room. Ascertaining the third floor, he climbed yet another narrow staircase leading to one of the manor's towers.

Within the lower portion of the pillar was an attic where James found two medium-sized chambers.

James was in a small attic chamber in the northwestern belfry. The sole window in the small room looked out onto a seemingly unending forest. These woods sprawled out over hills and valleys for miles to the north below. James surveyed every corner of the little room, yet he found nothing except some moth-eaten clothes and a heap of rusty jewelry sprawled on the floor. Evidently, the mysterious banging was coming from the adjacent room. This fact was confirmed as James opened the door to the second chamber.

This chamber was four steps higher than the first. As James closed the wooden door behind him, a whirl of dust enveloped his form. As he turned to enter the clanging became louder, seemingly emanating from the ceiling. As he stepped further the clanging abruptly stopped.

James saw a strange sight in one corner of the room—a large, ominous metal chest with a lit candle upon it, laying next to the only window. As the window was closed the room had no breeze, not even the slightest of any kind. Still, the candle flickered madly on top the metallic chest. James took a few paces toward the chest and removed the candle from the trunk. The candle's wax was cool to the touch.

He then lifted the cover of the metallic box, and using the wild, wavering light of the candle, he discovered two items. One was a long piece of knotted rope and the other a letter.

James began to read the letter now in his trembling hands.

Take heed upon reading this testimony, whomsoever shall find it, lest you also be cursed with the same grave and hopeless fate which has unhappily become my own. The baron is a devil, and the woman called Susan, the baroness, is a demon of the pit. All who dwell within this house are the property of Satan himself. No mitigating or moderating facts can lessen these awful truths. I trust in God's infinite justice that someday they shall be destroyed. But, as a prisoner here, I must release my soul in order to save it. And so, I must hang myself before it is too late. Sit pax anima mea in habitaculo justi. Amen.

James knew Latin well and therefore knew that this sentence translated into English was, "May my soul be at peace in the abode of the righteous."

The letter was signed at the paper's lower, right bottom in a sprawling hand.

Sir John Kenneth Dwight, 21 January 1353

At that moment, the light of the candle went completely out. A furious bolt of lightning crashed through the lone, large window, breaking its glass into countless pieces while illuminating the entire room. To his horror, James looked up and beheld a corpse hanging from the ceiling. The dead body swayed to and fro like a pendulous mast of a wild ship tossed by violent winds in a swirling storm. Its neck was tied with the same awful rope James found lying in the chest only a moment ago.

The head of the dead man dropped and looked down upon James as its eyes opened wide.

"So, there is no hell, James?" asked the dangling corpse.

James' throat was completely dry. In a state of despair he started stepping backwards and fell haphazardly out of the room and down the stone steps. He arose unhurt and ran screaming down the narrow corridor to a level partition on the highest floor.

James left the mad dead painter in the confines of the attic. After somehow finding his room, he almost immediately fell into a surreal and fitful sleep.   ☦

Chapter Eight
The Citadel

As the third night since James' arrival settled over Wycliff Manor, he wished among the cobwebs of his dreary bedroom that he had never come to such an accursed, haunted, and forsaken place.

"If only I had known! If only I had known!" James lamented as he sat on his bed beneath its elaborate canopy, thinking of what to possibly do next.

He must leave the house and leave as soon as possible. Rising from his bed, leaving his clothes in the dresser, he ran down two flights of stairs to the main hall from where he had first entered the mansion.

Wildly grasping the main door's metal knob in a panic, James tried to twist the knob open. But, unfortunately, in doing so, he hurt his wrist. To James' bitter disappointment, the great old door was firmly locked and bolted, seemingly from the outside. No bolts could be found on the door's oak interior.

James felt a chilling fear and despondency rush through his veins. In the enormous foyer, he collapsed into a chair next to the door and wept. James' chest commenced to heave as it became the victim of its doleful owner's heart-rending sobs. Eventually, in James' despair, he ceased crying, and his body grew calm. Yet, as his sobbing ceased, he heard a loud and wailing moan echoing through the estate.

Another succeeded this moan, and another, until the whole house became inundated with pitiful wailing. The appalling sounds seemed to be coming from the heights of the house, somewhere far above.

Enraged at what he perceived to be the newest threat to his existence, James was now determined to uncover the nature of the many black mysteries of the mansion no matter what the risk might be—if only to defend himself. Now that James understood he was a prisoner, he was compelled to disclose the intentions of the heinous beings behind these dark and manifold enigmas.

He flew up the same two stairways on which he had descended some moments before to attain the bastion's third and highest floor.

When James reached the top floor, he realized the moaning had died, and all had become silent. The ensuing silence was a thousand times more dreadful than the ghostly din of the hopeless wailing.

In the center of the manor, between its four towers, teeming high above the rest of the building, an immense oval-shaped citadel rose toward the sky. It was capped by a vast, weathered turquoise-hued dome of thick stained glass. James walked up a rocky stairwell to enter the enormous atrium.

He found many large wares containing antiquated soil with tawdry remains of dried, overgrown seedlings. In days of old, the monumental fortification must have served as a type of greenhouse since the many sprawling flower beds gave the huge amphitheater all the appearances of a vast potting shed.

In the omphalos of the oval bastion, a tall white statue stood on a lordly distinguished pedestal high above the citadel's floor. The noble-looking effigy was that of Aurelius Ambrosius, better known as Saint Ambrose, the fourth-century Bishop of Milan, who is still widely revered as an insightful biblical critic and a prominent doctor of the early Church. The figure was a copy of the seventeenth-century statue of the Saint in Museo del Duamo, Milan. As an erudite scholar, James recognized the copy at once and whom it represented. Gazing up at the majestic figure, James mused upon the many achievements of the celebrated holy man.

Suddenly, a precipitous and terrific bolt of lightning struck the center of the massive dome. The thunder accompanied by the bolt shook the floor beneath James' feet. The incredible thunder promptly shattered the whole of the rotunda's enormous glass roof. Suddenly, huge boxes of earth fell from enormous shelves with devastating violence. In an instant, the once regal grandeur of the citadel's ceiling was transformed into a shower of falling remnants of sharp speculum crashing like diamonds upon the marble floor.

James watched with disbelief as the statue
of Saint Ambrose became cryptically animated.
Fantastically, the sculpture took all the semblances of
a living being, just as the figure of Isis did the day prior in
the courtyard. Another flash of lightning coupled with
yet another tremendous rumble of thunder was
accompanied by a terrible expression of virulent hatred
on the face of the statue. As the floor of the wild cloister
shook, the spirited form of the now livid and
living Saint pointed its right finger directly at James.

It shouted with a blaring and sonorous tone of furious
indignation, "Yours is the soul of a long lost
reprobate, one whose heart knows no repentance!"

James went into shock. Losing all consciousness, he
collapsed on the tarnished marble floor.   ✝

Chapter Nine
The Terrace

Before taking the long meal with the James during his first night, the baron had introduced James to his room and the adjoining cluster of chambers on the western side of the mansion. The baron had told James that he might use these rooms to his liking, to study or rest in, or in any manner in which James saw fit. These rooms were positioned below one of the mansion's broad, tall towers on the southwestern corner of the immense and moribund medieval chateau.

With the exception of James' room (which was richly furnished, albeit worn, dusty, and dreary), the few chambers in that section of the mansion were profoundly drab, mostly empty, and distinctly haunted.

After the awful incident in the citadel, James awoke in his room the next morning. He had become conscious on the citadel's hard, unforgiving floor early that morning and, with some difficulty, found his way back to his bedroom. Now, sitting alone in his room recalling the events of previous night, he decided to explore the rooms two flights down and further north. On this fourth night in the mansion, James decided to not return to his dismal and desolate chambers beneath the southwestern tower.

Before exploring, he walked down to the dining room to get a quick breakfast. After finishing the lukewarm meal without any liking, devoid of the baron's company, James descended one of the more slender staircases he had noticed near the dining room. At the bottom, he walked the length of a dim, long hall. As he came to the first room on the left, James found its door locked from the inside.

Such was the case with the next two rooms. In the fourth cubicle, however, James found an open door.

Upon entering this niche, he first noticed its size and function. The room was monolithic displaying soft, bright-colored fabrics. In days of yesteryear, this room was ostensibly the grand bed chamber of an aristocratic lady. Long flowing curtains which lay against the windows were of the finest and most costly textiles, donned with elaborate white and purple frills. The bottom of their elegant ridges lay sprawling liberally upon the grand carpeted floor. As the windows behind the curtains were open to the night, the tapestries wavered in such a way that James became consumed with the idea that a ghostly and grim presence lurked somewhere among the circumvented drapes.

The room hosted only one bed, though its size was

prodigious, the bed ancient and elaborately decorated. The bed was splendid, dating back to the Middle Ages, featuring an ornate white canopy clad with long, manicured frills. Similar to the dreary, moth-eaten bed in James' room, this bed, although covered in dust, was otherwise in pristine condition.

Strangely enough, the carpet on the chamber floor betrayed fresh footprints on its thick coat of dust. By their shape, form, and size, the footprints were seemingly that of a woman's. Since the bedsheet was covered with a rich coat of dust, James could easily deduce that no one had slept in this bed for a very long time. Gazing down, James pensively asked, "How and why would fresh footprints be on the floor? And who made them?"

He began to regret this latest excursion to yet another dark and mysterious chamber in the dour immensity of the boundless estate, and felt it was best to leave at once rather than remain and learn its cryptic and foreboding secrets. As he turned toward the door, a breeze-borne whisper was released from the gap between the open windows. The cryptic whisper, carried on the late evening wind, uttered one word, "James …."

As James turned to the windows from where he heard his name, the long, white curtains suddenly flew open. With a perspicacious, peering glance, James could see that a sizable covered balcony lay beyond the open crevice. The curtains of the fissure were parted just enough for James to behold the ancient stonework of the terrace.

A loud and fiendish laugh came from the drafty opening of the hanging edifice. Then, upon the terrace, James beheld the form of a ghostly and gruesome-looking woman. Although he could not see the woman's as it loomed in the shadowy recess, the horrid figure spoke.

"James, your nights are numbered here."

James concluded that this ghostly woman was a daughter of the evil one. Determined to ambush James as if to claim his soul, the foul thing stepped into the room. James turned and ran for the exit. As he did so, he could hear the curtain violently being torn into several long shreds. As the drapes were thrown to the floor, the mysterious and malevolent maiden entered, walking disjointedly toward James.

Looking back, James caught the sight of her pale, dead hand holding a knife. He fled with incredible speed up to the third floor and ascertained the relative safety of his bedchamber which he had formerly considered unsafe harbor.

Promptly, James Asher, Junior collapsed upon the dust of his bed and fainted. ✝

Chapter Ten
The Hallway

Since his arrival at Wycliff Manor, James had been suffering from an initial state fear that grew to a mounting state of fear. That initial burgeoning trepidation had grown into a severe and ever present state of despair. The fifth evening of James' residence in the old house had arrived.

A completely hidden moon shrouded by a thick sheet of misty clouds covered the environs of Wiltshire, cloaking the turrets of the manor as if with a nebulous veil reserved for the dead. James had slept poorly. With nightmares of ghosts and demons dominating his tormented psyche, he continued sleeping through most of the day. During his slumber, a dense and ghostly gray fog flushed the entire edifice of Wycliff Manor.

Each cell of the mansion, large and small, along with every hall and crevice, were immersed in the creeping mist. The vast exterior perimeter of the manor seemed to be inundated with the enveloping vapor. No birds ceased singing in the wavering trees surrounding the estate.

Otherworldly billows of ill gloom permeated the castle and its grounds. For miles around, a malevolent silence dominated the forests and dales forming an intangible wreath of death around the house like a circular funeral pyre. The dank, thick, cold air clung to the manor's countless walls as a lonely dog wailed somewhere far off in the southern wood.

Against his better judgement, James found himself wandering once more through the many rooms and corridors of the black, old bastion. Wycliff Manor was an immense and gloomy prison from which James was seeking an alternative exit as the main entry continued to be secured by unearthly means.

At the far end of the now foggy main dining room, James discovered an ornate wooden door. This aperture was encased within an arched Romanesque column of large time-weathered stones. On each side of this door, laden with a plethora of rusted iron nails, stood two regal busts made of exceptionally fine marble. Each bust was seated on an ivory-hued pedestal, also made of marble. The two persons depicted by the august busts were of high-ranking social echelons in their time. They were both of noble grandeur and each expressed an air of royalty.

One of these sculptures was of King Edward III, as a rusted plate of gold below the bust spelled out his name. The other bust, to the left, whose name plate was too worn to be deciphered, was of a woman who, in life, was evidently also a regal figure, as she wore a splendidly molded aureole.

James pushed open the large door and found it swung back in its casement rather smoothly. What he did not expect to see was the long, dark hallway in which he now found himself. As James peered into the abysmal darkness the passageway seemed endless. The only light James could perceive came from a distant lancet window at the far end. The little bit of moonlight issuing through the opening was obscured by the nebulous haze permeating each and every corner of the house.

With grave reservation, James decided to explore the grim looking aisle, hoping he could find an accessible way out of the nightmarish place. James' boots caused his footsteps to ring heavily on the stone-paved floor.

Without warning, a hand from a black recess grabbed James' leg with a mighty force. James let out a scream and tried to free himself from the grip of the mysterious being. In a moment's flash, a candelabra fastened to the wall became brightly inflamed by an enigmatic force.

The lights from the candles revealed a horrid corpse emerging from the floor, its hands still clasped tightly around James' right leg. He saw the flesh of the corpse's head and hand was partially eaten, revealing a portion of its skull and bones. James struggled with ineffable fear as the corpse began to cry in a pitiful voice of anguish and despair.

"Help me back to earth! Oh, help me! Help me! Help me! Give me one more chance to prove God's justice was wrong in damning me!"

Terrible as it was, the hideous being was then

swallowed by the stony floor which had opened to assume it. To James' immeasurable terror, he witnessed the inexorable tier of the floor mend itself, completely encasing the ghoul. The last dreadful glimpse James had of the assumed body was its twisted face betraying a countenance entirely devoid of all hope...   ✝

Chapter Eleven
The Library

In the confines of the vast and haunted manor, the only aspects of life experienced by James were a black, horrid malevolence and profound sense of a diabolic mystery. Indeed, since James had arrived at Wycliff, all he had come to know were the manifold realms of virulence, darkness, and incessant gloom.

James felt all the suffocating trappings of a hopeless prisoner during his nightly dinners with Baron Von Drake. After these meals, as soon as the baron would leave James alone in the massive dining hall, he would explore different regions of the dilapidated palace. He did so primarily to find any possible egress through which he could escape.

James' secondary motive for exploring the many nooks of the castle was to feel more like a man who was still remotely blessed with the privileges of freedom.

On James' sixth evening at Wycliff Manor, after his experience in the dining room's hidden hallway, he was walking down the main corridor to the great hall of portraits beyond main wide staircase. At the end of the hall, directly across from each other, were two large wooden doors with a stone-framed window open to the moonlight. The slender window couldn't accommodate a human being and was high over the forested ground.

James first tried the door on his right. As it gave way, he discerned an immense, stately chamber. This lodging featured four remarkable knights, one in each corner of the recess, standing clad in suits of armor. They were somewhat rusted though still splendid to the sight.

In the center of the cubicle lay a vast oak podium where, in times of old no doubt, regal courts conducted public affairs and planned adventurous conquests of foreign lands. Many colorful emblems, dating back to the fourteenth and fifteenth centuries, of England and its empire hung high on the teeming brick walls of the cell. Hovering above a magnificent stone hearth behind the huge oak table was Wiltshire's great coat of arms with its fierce-looking red lion painted against a green and white background.

In the center of the chamber, one refined chandelier was perched high above the bureau. This light fixture was most likely, in its time, certainly a wondrous and stunning object to behold. Still, in its antediluvian condition, it radiated a mystic aura of regalia even though it bore no lights and was covered with thick sheets of cobwebs—dead as a stone, it seemed. James looked up at the grand corona with quiet admiration.

As James gazed with wonder at the chandelier, it slowly began to move in a circular motion. James thought a formidable wind must be stirring at the top of the chamber to cause the mysterious rotation. Yet he observed the flags hanging high on the bulwarks remained completely still.

Indeed James perceived no movement in the air until, enigmatically, the chandelier suddenly began to twirl in a fit like a tornado accompanied by moans and groans. The lamentations seemed to radiate from the spinning light fixture as spirits who possessed no hope nor the slightest chance of reclamation for their lost and banished souls. James ran out of the room across the hall into the hallway's second chamber.

Within this recess, he found a vast library stocked with endless volumes of dusty old books. In this library was situated one enormous, continual bookshelf, extending to all four walls framing the entire room. In the middle of the library lay another large bureau with many scrambled papers resting on its wooden surface… a considerable collection of books, essays, and varied periodicals.

As James approached the table to survey the material, one of the larger books on a shelf behind him fell to the floor from high in the corner of the gallery descending with a loud thud.

Looking at the book, James bent down to pick it up. He turned to the tome's dusty front cover—it was the King James version of the Holy Bible. An instant later, a mysterious power in the form of a cryptic breeze opened the Bible to a page in the New Testament. James read the inscription from scripture underlined with a sanguine reddish pigment:

"Then Jesus demanded, 'What is your name?'

And he replied, 'My name is Legion because there are many of us inside this man.'"

Familiar with the scriptural passage, James knew Satan was the being who had answered the Lord's question. In a state of fright, James threw the holy book onto the floor. To his amazement, the entire Bible became ablaze with a demonic glow inflamed in a hellish fire.

The next moment, its tattered pages ascended into the wild air as bits of pulpy embers. As he had heard the night before in the terrible hallway, a ghastly laugh once more emanated from the walls around him. Only this laughter was a thousand times more sinister than the previous night, born of a saturnine, angelic being. This baleful entity owned an empty, envious, metallic voice and possessed a proud and merciless soul.

At once, James knew the angel's name was Lucifer…

James flew out of the library, down the hall, and up the stony staircase to the sanctuary of his room. Yet as he slammed shut his bedroom door, he could still hear the demon's laughter far below echoing through the desolate halls.   ✞

Chapter Twelve
The Bell Tower

On James' seventh night at Wycliff, after another fitful sleep, he awoke late afternoon in a state of dread. Alighting from his bed he dressed in haste and left his chamber

After grabbing a bite to eat, James began exploring a corridor adjacent to his bedroom. At the end of the hall, he began ascending a shallow stairway to find himself in another one of the mansion's tall, prodigious towers. This tower was on the northwestern corner of the mansion.

Two enormous metal bells hung from a wooden plank directly above James' head. From three of the tower's four brick walls were the stuffed heads of several beasts projecting inwards. The air was foul and musty. A throng of diseased, rancid rats scurried across the filthy old floor.

James was not alone.

The enormous bells above James' head began ringing, moving to and fro with a ghostly sway. The bells began to ring violently, echoing louder and louder through the chamber. Soon enough, they ceased to move altogether.

This belfry featured three arched openings. Each had its base five feet above the mortar and stone of the ancient floor. Dust particles could be seen where muted sunlight streamed through the apertures. Large, concentric cobwebs framed each corner of the tower, high above, amid the bells. A worn and weathered coat of arms hung beside each of the belfry's three vertical openings.

Outside, several teeming, sprawling branches rose to the height of the apertures devoid of glass. These towering boughs had their origins in several outgrowths which grew skyward from the many crevices of the castle's walls far below.

James looked up through one of the openings and beheld an early evening crescent moon encircled by fleeting clouds as the firmament was beset with winds. In the midst of the branches, the contorted faces and forms of many demons suddenly appeared in the mystic twilight. James was terrified as he peered into the bloody, scarlet orbs of the demons' lifeless eyes.

Without warning, one of the devils flew off the bough on which he was sitting and passed through one of the windows to clasp James' throat. James struggled to breathe but did so to no avail as the demon's grip grew tighter. Its eyes were of a piercing, fiery red; its form was black. The devil stared into James' eyes with unadulterated hatred.

With its hand wrapped around James' neck, the demon lifted James high up off the floor and spoke, "Do you really think after what you have done that you can ever escape us?"

James could hear maddening laughter from the other devils perched on the branches outside. Then, with a look of utter disdain, using its terrible and mighty arm, the demon threw James upon the stony floor and departed through the window from which it had entered.   ✞

Chapter Thirteen
The Ballroom

More than a week after James arrived at the villa, the weather became balmy for the first time. Regardless, a thick dank moisture still clung to the castle walls.

Still in the bell tower, James woke from a deep coma in a daze, his right arm sorely aching. Taking a few minutes to regain his composure, he struggled to his feet and took a long time to gaze out the window from where he had been accosted. James decided to leave the belfry.

He found a way down the main hall to a medium-sized study. Within this den were two finely constructed bureaus made of the costliest timber. James could see no windows save upon the chamber's slanted roof, a portion of its ceiling open to the sky.

Lifting his head to gaze at the elliptical-shaped opening, James beheld the stars and wished he had never made this awful excursion to the wilds of Wiltshire. Pining for a way out of the ancient, grim place, James longed with a heavy heart to be home in his beloved town of Boston.

As he was musing on these thoughts, he heard, from a distant chamber, the sobbing reverberation of a solemn cello, slowly and gravely playing the opening coda from the Canon in D by the German composer and organist Johann Pachelbel. The haunting aria filled James with a wondrous sense of awe.

In the immediate hall, the languorous strain could be heard more distinctly, only now nimbly accompanied by a violin. The haunting canticle became decisively louder, saturating every recess of the corridor, as if a ghost permeated its ethereal spaces.

In the passage where James now stood, the long corridor led to the room from where the music originated. The melody was issuing forth from the far western wing of the manor's second story. And as James was walking down this second foyer, a French horn commenced wistfully, high above the cello and violin. In the space of a few moments, James attained the alcove from where the symphonic refrain was enigmatically progressing.

He opened the grand door and entered the chamber to behold an immense and magnificent ballroom. Far above his head, a throng of golden, lit, shining chandeliers glistened from the shimmer of a thousand candles.

The floor was made of the finest oak. Several splendid ivory statues, all made of the finest alabaster, graced each corner of the vast bastille. The tune grew even louder as a flute and harpsichord blended with the remainder of the rapturous air. Yet as James discerned the entirety of the room, he saw no musicians nor instruments of any kind.

He continued scrutinizing every sector of the vast ballroom, yet not another soul was to be seen within the immense amphitheater. Yet, the music played on…

A colossal painting of what appeared to be of the manor itself hung on one of the teeming walls of the dance hall. Only this painting depicted Wycliff Manor with a lively, bright, lustrous character. The colorful mural was rectangular in shape and situated between various plates of armor.

As James looked on with wonder at the painting, the music began to retard terribly. The melodious symphony transformed into a dissonant strain of inharmonious clatter. The infernal din became monstrous as the pigments of the painting began to bleed off its canvass.

James looked on with terror as those horrid oils descended to the floor, blood-red. He left the ballroom and returned to his chamber to get some rest.   ✿

Chapter Fourteen
The Graveyard

Nine nights transpired since James had arrived at Wycliff Manor; yet he had made no progress on his work and had not met his cousin Susan.

He thought it more than curious that he had not yet even seen the woman who invited him to the mansion. Whenever he inquired about the whereabouts of his cousin, the baron's reply was unwavering, "She is away in Manchester tending to her ill mother." Now that almost a fortnight had transpired since he had been welcomed to the cryptic palace, James was terrified beyond his wildest imagination.

"Surely," James thought, "Susan, by now, must know I am in England and here at the mansion. Why did she summon me to England in the first place?"

The invitation to Wycliff baffled James. It was a mystery James could not brook. As Susan was nowhere to be seen, he could no longer believe that the motive for the invitation was friendly, one in which he could meet his cousin and work on his dissertation. Instead, James began to feel deep down that behind his cousin's invitation existed an ulterior and ill intention.

The dark and strange events that had transpired in the forsaken place caused James to become more and more distressed. He was beginning to feel aghast just looking at the very walls of the manor—as if James were languishing within a hellish domain trapped in a dismal and dreary dream.

On its vast, sallow hill, Wycliff Manor was quite isolated on three sides from any other distinguished place of notice. To the north and south (beyond the southern square and its few tombs) lay miles of coniferous forest. The only exceptions were medium-sized courtyards to the east and south, with a very small cemetery consisting of only three tombs remaining among the latter. Beyond the main square to the east lay dales and woodlands leading to Tilshead, over two full miles away. Yet, twenty yards to the west was the entrance to a vast and ancient graveyard visible from the manor's southwest belfry.

James' bedroom was just below this very same tower which had two windows, each looking west. Both were set in arched stone encasements and were identical in size and form. From the opening on the right, several small boughs of a towering treetop tapped menacingly upon the panes, as though an invisible hand was moving them to and fro in the accursed odiousness of the night.

Yet when James looked out from his bedroom window to the left no trees obscured his view. He could see the entrance to the graveyard as well as a good portion of the remainder of the cemetery.

On this night, the moon was not obscured and the manor was strangely still, more so than ever before. A heavy wind began to blow into James' bedroom chamber. This wind was the only sound to be heard as it moaned from the direction of the cemetery far below. As he stood gazing out and down upon the remote and archaic place, James could view most of the graveyard's area.

The graveyard itself had been neglected for centuries. Almost every headstone was broken. The few crypts standing near the cemetery's entrance were covered with a thick, sickly greenish moss. The yew trees near the ogive swayed ominously in the howling winds blowing from the west. Aside from the moans of these winnowing breezes, the only other movement James could detect from his perch was the swaying of many tall blades of grass. Their wavering tops wrapped around the bases of the crypts. Still, no sound could heard except for the wailing wind.

The moonlight had a tranquilizing effect on James, and he decided to lie down on his bed. After about an hour, he fell into a deep sleep.

All at once a collective chorus of moans arose from the graveyard. These moans quickly became mixed with occasional sharp wailing sounds. The cacophony was loud enough to awaken James from his heavy slumber.

"The witches' hour has arrived"—such was James' thought.

The moaning and wailing continued. Now on his feet, James was looking out his window, intently watching and listening. The sounds emanating from the voices seemed to carry forth from souls bereft of hope.

Unfettered moonlight illuminated the graveyard. Although the pitiful cries came from the cemetery, James could see no one. He struggled to witness as much of the cemetery as he possibly could. The light from the cloudless firmament now illuminated the entire graveyard as if lit by powerful spotlights.

At once the moaning and wailing ceased, and an awful silence swept across the land as far as the eye could see. The wind ceased to blow and the trees became still. The barren boughs on the western side of the house were now motionless—as if the world had died.

James felt his heart pound madly as he peered into the moonlit distance, searching to witness the strange, wild cause for the moaning and wailing. Far into the cemetery, between the tombstones, yew trees, and crypts, James could see a dim white figure passing slowly over the grasses and the dead, tall reeds.

The mysterious figure was heading toward the cemetery. As it drew closer, James could see the figure of a woman wearing a burial shroud! The long, tattered, and torn shroud ran to the woman's bare feet—her face was chalky, pallid, and deathly pale. Her hair was raven black, caked with dirt and wet leaves.

As she reached the entrance to the graveyard, she stopped walking to look up. She spoke not a word, standing still as a statue, unmoving and unmoved.

James was astonished as he realized he was beholding an animated corpse. Overcome with the horror of it all, he fell from the bedroom window to the floor below. ✞

Chapter Fifteen
The Music Room

The following day, James came to very late in a nebulous state finding himself dressed and lying prostrate on the bedroom floor. A yellowish, dim sun had dawned over Wycliff Manor.

Since James had traveled from Boston to Tilshead, he had come to feel that Wycliff Manor possessed a life of its own, that it was not merely an edifice made of stone, brick, and mortar but the whole of the dreadful place was itself a living soul—an ominous soul. What was even more prescient in James' mind was that Wycliff Manor embodied a murderous and vengeful soul.

James was profoundly shaken after the events of the previous night. He was fervently hoping that the horrid happenings which had apparently transpired were merely the product of a terrible dream. Yet he knew in his heart and mind that it was all grim and stark reality.

"What kind of place was this that he had come to?

Among what kind of people had fate cast him?
Among what kind of creatures did he now dwell?"

These burning questions tortured James' psyche as he attempted to sustain the remainder of his reason.

He washed his face in a metal basin and combed his hair with shaking hands. Then, he dared to curiously look out the bed chamber window.

James could see no one and nothing out of the ordinary, neither in the cemetery nor anywhere else in the area below. Perplexed, he decided to explore more of the manor with the intention of leaving at his first opportunity.

At the eastern side of the mansion, adjacent to the courtyard, James could not hear any larks chirping in the bowers although it was now mid-afternoon. He had not yet explored this portion of the mansion nor the rooms above the gardens.

As the sky had become completely cloudless, the sun morphed from a weak, yellow hue into a bold, golden throng of summery rays. These powerful glowing streams of light began to boldly sift through the windows.

James opened several doors and looked into two medium-sized rooms, yet he could see nothing in them of notice (aside from dust-laden furniture and a few large desks made of oak and mahogany). In the third room, however, he found a pine desk of such elegant design, he decided to explore its contents. Within the second drawer from the top, James found a letter written in Medieval rhyme.

The poem was entitled *The Music Room.*

Moaning reverberates within the halls;
Candles flicker eerily on cold, stone walls.
Behind an old bookshelf souls do plea
Where they are engraved
To be set free.
Yet no one shall be saved
Within these castellated towers
Nor shall they behold the florid, golden bowers
Of the merciful sun—
No—no one.
For within one chamber a piano plays;
Its keys are caressed by ghostly fingers
In the ancient parlor where a melody lingers,
A nebulous hymn of stony grays
Floating on the air to the window's veil.
The musician, once lovely, is now deathly pale.
Why does it seek me, this concerto of gloom
Which fades on the glades beneath the room?
Who is this wraith who wears the face
Of the husband I knew in a happier time
When I would weave my sunlit rhyme
So very very long ago
In the bright, sweet boons of a summery place?
I am haunted by the tune he plays with grace
Now, as then,
Dying on the dales below

On the reedy, dismal glen
Through the dreadful, dark haze of the half opened window…

The poem was signed, *To My Dearest Edward, Yours forevermore, Philippa.*

In the fourth and final chamber, James made another, more fantastic discovery. This room was significantly larger than the proceeding three and possessed an airy, summery, almost cheerful glow. Positioned right above the center of a vast bower of multicolored blooms, briars, hedgerows, roses, and other various flora, the chamber had a tall, grand bay window opening directly above the center of the garden on the far front wall. As James cautiously crossed the threshold and proceeded to close the door behind him, he heard a delightful strain of music.

This mysterious melodic air seemed as though it were being played near the sunny bay window branching out above the flowery bower some fifteen feet below. The melody was poignant and sweet. Most impressive was that the music was being played on a fine grand piano by a most gifted and cunning hand. As James approached the ostensible source of the music, he changed his mind, convinced it was coming from a sunny corner of the room on the other side of the chamber where he could almost see the silhouette of a piano.

As James approached, the melody continued filling the room with its own unique and beautiful sentiments—

those of a love's purity now lost. The lovely, wistful tune seemed to gracefully flow out the grand bay's half-opened window down the wall into the garden below.

James could glimpse the tops of overgrown vines which had entered the room covering another large window's lattice, profusely sprawling down the wall. To James, the emerald vines trailing down the wall to the garden were like a banished woman's outstretched hands reaching for her banished lover. Suddenly, as James approached the corner of the chamber where the piano came into focus, the music abruptly and completely ceased.

Lifting his eyes to look upon the splendid instrument, James was shocked to behold no one sitting on the piano bench. Neither was there another human being to be seen within the entire room. In the next moment, to James' absolute dismay, the piano keys were struck with such a force that James could feel the floor of the entire cabin shake beneath his feet. He heard a loud, discordant chord blare from the instrument, encircling the entire room with dissonant vibrations. As James stood in disbelief, he watched the piano keys violently move up and down entirely devoid of human hands or fingers.

A mad, grisly hymn emerged from the piano, swaying the enormous diadems above James' head to and fro like hapless ships tossed by unbridled waves in a hostile storm. The abhorrent carol became louder still, more furious and discordant.

Then, above the distorted hymn, dark demonic laughter began to expand and rise filling the whole of the haunted chamber. As the quaking vibrations of the mad cacophony propelled objects off the mantelpiece lining one wall of the crazy cubicle, James ran for the door by which he had entered.

As James escaped through the doorway, he heard the door slam behind him so hard and mercilessly that, when he looked back, he could see the door's frame had splintered.

Retreating to a medium-sized room on the upper floor, James hid under a settee for the remainder of the day, much as a terrified child hides beneath the mantle of his mother. In a few hours, night fell.

James had become accustomed to the loathsome, varied oddities of the dreadful chambers and hallways in the boundless estate. Winds blew hard and cold through the seemingly endless rooms and hallways. Strangely enough, where there was no wind, candles flickered madly on the old stone walls. Hinges could be heard creaking in doorless recesses. Curtains swayed ominously in every cell wherever they were to be seen.

James could hear enigmatic moaning and groaning from the bowels of the manor, as if tortured souls were imprisoned in the abhorrent vaults of the mansion's netherworld.

From the castellated towers, moonlight bled from high above to be reflected into the manor's uppermost enclosures. As the gleaming light descended into the manor's apertures, it took on the glow of a glistening mist, throwing long, phantom forms upon the fortification's tawdry floors. The countless corridors of the mansion embraced only mysteries. Every virulent aspect of the world's most malevolent and ominous evils found their lurid homes in the blackest corners of the bastion's hallways.

As the evening began to cover the estate, James extracted himself from the dusty niche beneath the sofa. He found that both his hands were shaking violently and decided to make another desperate attempt to escape the prison of Wycliff.

The nascent night arose with billows of black and moaning tempests, and an egregious cold trailed down from the gloom of the third and second floors to the main stairway leading to the foyer. Descending on the flanks of the ancient stone steps, James felt the howling gale's terrible chill. Desperately hoping to find the main door unlocked, he lunged at its metal knob. It was firmly secured. Regardless of how hard James pulled, the door would not move. That's when James heard a furious pounding from the other side of the old oak door. His heart jumped until the pounding was succeeded by a chorus of screams from the damned of the dead.

"Let us in!" one soul cried.

"Where do you come from?" James inquired.

"From the blackness of the graves and tombs!"

Terrified, James ran up the two flights of stairs once more into the murky, relative safety of his own dark and dismal chamber. ✠

Chapter Sixteen
The Tomb

The night was when innumerable malignancies of the vast old house and its grounds held their strongest sway. Yet even in the afternoons when the yellow sun lingered above the courtyards and ponds, the notion that malicious beings were wandering the grounds with murderous intentions was still easy to apprehend. Such an appreciation came into the mind of anyone who surveyed the grim details of the area.

At dusk, the entire edifice of Wycliff Manor took on a terrible glow where no earthly light illuminated the property. Rather, in James' mind, the only gleam came from the eyes of demons seeking to ensnare souls of the living, for it was just as night would thicken over the immense estate when James would see their translucent forms prowl through the heights of the dismal house. In the black towers of the manor, only the most diabolical minds and their retinue would freely choose to go.

James decided to return to the foyer, for he knew he

had to escape regardless of the ghosts without. Running downstairs to the manor's mammoth front hall, he eagerly laid his hand on the knob of the great oak door. To his stark surprise James found the door unlocked, for as he pulled the door toward him it moved backward in the threshold. He ran outside with a feeling of freedom he had not known since arriving in Wiltshire. Invigorated with the sudden rush of newfound liberty flowing through his blood, James needed to escape the mansion while the opportunity was at hand.

James' boots rang out on the stones in front of the house as a strong easterly breeze swept over his face, now dripping with sweat. He decided to leave the manor from a different direction than he had originally approached hoping to elude the baron and all other loathsome creatures, should any decide to follow.

As he surveyed the vast eastern entryway of the bastion, he knew this direction beyond the main square over the dales and streams was where his former path lay from Tilshead. To baffle any would-be followers, James left the confines of the cloister turning right to the southern courtyard instead of the known path. He meant to discover another means through the southern wilderness to the sanctuary of any town or village.

The evening sky was clear, almost turquoise; the stars seemed close to the earth glimmering, easy for James to distinguish. As he sauntered through the ruins of the ancient square, he peered beyond to a reedy dale south of the estate where the yellow grasses were tall, slender, and pale.

Suddenly a wayward breeze spoke of a solemn and impending dread. The entire glade housed only the dead; the trees were bereft of any leaves. James could see a rectangular reedy field where bare oak trees stood behind one of the ancient, cloudy ponds on the southern end of the manor's grounds, touching the edge of the courtyard.

Immediately beyond that dale was a dark, dense, seemingly endless forest. Yet, most disturbing about this field was that it housed three graves, all constructed above ground, perched high over the reedy floor. Each of these age-old crypts was made of moss-covered stone. The stones, in turn, were clothed by an overgrowth of sun-parched vines.

As James approached, a pungent, horrid odor of perpetually decaying flesh permeated the area. Instead of crosses commemorating the bodies buried in these crypts, no symbols could be seen. Two names on the crypts could not be discerned, as time coupled with the elements had washed them away. Yet, as James approached, he could see a name still visibly chiseled on the third and closet sepulcher. The name engraved was Roger Mortimer, etched high upon a pale, white concrete slab that topped the crypt.

James continued walking through the field until he heard a groan discharge from the grave marked Mortimer. Stopping in his tracks, he was shocked as he looked back at the sepulcher. Its ancient gate opened and a skeletal hand, half-clothed with flesh, clad in a ripped, dark sleeve, wrapped around the rim of the tomb's vine-clad door. And from that abhorrent and odious chamber,

a more fantastic scene emerged. As the gate opened
wider, the entire ghastly and appalling figure of Roger
Mortimer, the murderer of King Edward II, stepped out
into the world once again.

His eyes were redder than blazing coals oozing with
the essence of animistic hunger; his face was pallid and
waxen. Dressed in a torn, black suit, the deceased began
to race haphazardly toward James.

James promptly reversed his steps and flew toward the
courtyard. It had rained the night before, and as James
neared the marble square, he slipped on yellow reeds of
the square's marble border, hitting his head hard on the
unforgiving stones. The next thing James knew,
Mortimer's animated corpse had grabbed both legs and
was pulling him away from the courtyard in the direction
of Mortimer's tomb!

Dazed and barely conscious from his fall, James came
to his full senses within the black confines of the enclosed
sepulcher. The dead, oily mouth of Mortimer began to
speak in a rusty, raspy voice.

"So! You do not care for my company? Nor do you
care for my hospitality or for the comforts of my home?
Are you not indeed a fiend like I? Are you not indeed
a murderer?"

Letting out a scream, James kicked open the heavy
door of the large stone tomb. Mortimer spewed out a
bitter and repulsive cackle from his pale mouth as James

fled from the gruesome receptacle, tumbling over the grass, running toward the courtyard.

James glanced back to see Mortimer following in pursuit. With great strength and speed, James lifted the head of a fallen disembodied statue and flung it at the fast-approaching carrion. The object met Mortimer's chest with a formidable impact, bouncing off the dead man's body as it swirled to the grassy ground. The deceased fell upon the reeds as James raced beyond the courtyard through the cloister to the main door of the mansion.

In a great fit of panic, he swiftly pushed the ingress open to enter the manor's foyer. Now in the main hall, James bolted the mighty door shut. James' psyche spun in a sea of stars for several minutes—he simply could not believe what just transpired. Gradually, he began to feel genuine gratitude for having attained the bastion's interior in a state of relative safety once more. For there, within the hall, as loathsome as it was to James, no signs of crypts and tombs with their manifold horrors existed…

Yet just as James was standing in the foyer, he heard the same piano playing in the music room one flight up, just as he had heard it in that same hall two days prior. Tonight's performance was a melancholic yet lively concerto that seemed to issue forth from the grounds of a ghostly carnival. The music seeped like a torrent of blood oozing down the foyer's walls from the height of the music room. In a rage without hesitation, James ran up the circular staircase and flew into the room where the melody originated.

As James entered the music ceased and no soul was to be seen. In the silence, a potent and mysterious tempest threw open the huge bay window, its curtains eerily swaying in from over the garden. James walked over to look through the window, only to behold the figure of Roger Mortimer staring blindly up at him from the bower below. Another Orphic breeze parted the curtains further and the sanguine scent of death flooded the chamber with unhallowed air.

"Take one step forward from that height. If you believe in God, He will save you from death and ruin!" Mortimer cajoled.

James felt deep in his soul a cruel temptation to fling his body over the parapet—a wicked, burning desire to cast his body into the abyss. Yet he realized that in yielding to the monster's cruel temptation, he would only accomplish his death. He saw the dead man's smirking grin with a look of diabolic expectation on its hungry face. By this time, James was on fire with the desire to escape the mansion at any cost. So extreme was James' longing to escape; his mind was bordering on derangement. The deceased being knew this and was exploiting this urgency in James to be rid of all of his trouble—by snatching his immortal soul.

The dead man looked into James' eyes with a searing hatred. That's when James became enraged and screamed, "What is the meaning of this accursed place? Who in heaven's name are you? What is the meaning of all of this madness?"

Before the spectre could answer, James withdrew from the window. Closing the door to the music room shut, he fled in a state of utter terror down the hall.   ☦

Chapter Seventeen
The Sepulcher

Two days after the incident at the tomb, dawn turned into a dim light of morning over Wycliff Manor, when the sun was typically at its brightest. On this morn, a dark, gray sky covered the bleak and boundless estate. A tepid, balmy day was dawning over the mansion. Nevertheless, bold, gold sunlight streamed through the clouds and windows into James' ancient bed chamber.

As James awoke, he heard a piano playing again somewhere downstairs. Enraged and determined to investigate, he hastily dressed to leave his room. At once, the piano ceased. Frustrated and bewildered, James sat back on his ornate bed. Reluctantly, he reclined upon its mattress. Morning turned into afternoon, and James realized he had once again fallen asleep—he was still fully dressed, wearing his boots.

Suddenly, from out of the darkness of his room, in a fantastic and mystical manner, James was transported body and soul to a splendid veranda at the rear of the castle, not far from the cemetery. The veranda was circular, simply constructed, and made of gleaming linden wood.

From the base of the veranda to its ornate roof, the structure was graced with vines and various blooms heavenly in form and rich with a pristine light no words could decipher. Descending gracefully down through the belvedere's canopy, a beautiful virgin adorned with a glistening aura spread her fair, white hands graciously extending them to James. She looked at James with eyes full of mercy, smiling with only peace and forgiveness.

"I am the Immaculate Conception," the woman spoke in an angelic voice that called songbirds and doves down from the highest heaven, transcending all sweetness. "Confess your sins, my son, and your soul shall be freed from the chains of this accursed place. For to remain here shall certainly lead to your perdition!"

Defiant, James remained obstinate in silence. He spoke not a word, and turned away from the woman, his face still and grave as stone.

At this, the beautiful woman's countenance expressed deep and solemn sadness. Then in a moment's time, the woman and the veranda completely disappeared and a throng of demons suddenly roamed the grounds and filled the dale with desperate dread—only the night could hear the words they said.

And the once bright sky became an infernal red. The heavens became darker than night as the winds in the heights of the firmament began to carry sheets of black clouds devoid of haziness, devoid of all light.

In the next moment, James was once more spiritually transported, this time back to his bed in the loathsome prison of his shadowy room. He was still fully dressed, donning his boots, when from out of the darkness of the ghostly chamber he heard a raspy, horrid voice exclaim, "What appropriate attire for a burial!"

Two demons began to laugh. In the following instant, James felt a pair of hands drag him off the bed out of the room and down the main hall.

As he struggled to open his eyes, he could see he was being ushered down the staircase through the foyer out into the cloister. As James was again being dragged through the ruined courtyard, he opened his eyes wide. To his horror he beheld two demonic figures, one on either side of him. The two devils were transporting his body around the mansion's perimeter in the graveyard's direction.

Attaining the entrance to the cemetery, the demons, with their human cargo in hand, began laughing louder. James began screaming, but his pleas for help were to no avail. The strength of the demonic grip which held him in a frozen posture was incomparable.

As James was carried into the depths of the cemetery, he looked downward, his mouth agape. To his left, he saw a freshly dug grave with an open coffin made of boxwood on the grassy floor. In concert, the two demons lifted James' body high into the air and slammed it down brutally on the grass.

James lost all consciousness. One minute passed. When he awoke, he found his body interred in the boxwood coffin and he could see nothing but darkness as the coffin was sealed. He heard a loud thud slam against the roof, succeeded by another and another. The sounds were piles of soil thrown down upon the coffin. He was being buried alive.

Too horrified to scream, his ability to breathe was becoming impossible as the oxygen in the crate was speedily diminishing. In an act of abject desperation, he pushed with all his might upward against the lid of the suffocating crate. James was a man of incredible strength. To his great relief the casket cracked open. As it did, a stream of musty soil seeped into the crate, half engulfing his body.

Opening the lid of the coffin wide enough to squeeze through, James took a deep breath, held it, and was somehow able to swim through the mound of loose soil, eventually attaining the top of the soil's heap at ground level. Pulling his body over the rim of the grass above, he extracted himself from the grave.

Seeing James' progress, the two demons attempted to cast him back into the grave's orifice. But with great alacrity, James flew around both of them escaping their clutches. He ran toward the estate grounds into the great mansion and up to his room.   ✚

Chapter Eighteen
The Dining Room

As the joyless days of May waned into the dreary afternoons of June, an inexplicable chill permeated the chambers and hallways of Wycliff Manor. In contrast to the remainder of England, which was becoming decidedly more tepid, the weather encircling Wycliff and its environs grew inexplicably colder.

Hinges were heard to creak in chambers devoid of doors. The sound of moans came forth from behind solid walls as if the souls of the damned were imprisoned therein. In the many trees surrounding the house, no songbirds sang. With each sallow dawn, the sun's rays became more listless. The only penetrative light came from a soulless, haunted moon—as if the whole of Wycliff Manor was constructed and sustained by a collective, dark, and demonic funeral pyre.

In the first week of the new month of June, James and the baron had quietly taken their nightly meal in the gigantic dining room. At the baron's suggestion, both men took seats next to the chamber's regal fireplace to smoke cigars.

Tonight, James noticed an evil gleam in the baron's eye. He appeared lost in nebulous thoughts. After several minutes of total silence in which neither man spoke, James felt the solemn reticence unbearable. Snuffing out his cigar, he asked the baron, "I assume this house and its estate have always been in possession of the Drake family name?"

"Ah, yes!" the baron replied with a lively smile. "Since the construction of this house was completed, it was ceded into the hands of one of my forefathers... A gift, you see, from the reigning monarch at the time, King Edward III, to the paternal line of the Drakes. Of course, King Edward never gave the estate entirely away, for he often used this house as his main bastion during the Hundred Years' War against the French. Seizing the crown after the criminal, Roger Mortimer, stole it from Edward's father, Edward nailed Mortimer to a huge pine slab on the grounds of this house. Although the dishonorable thief did not liken himself to the character of Saint Peter, he was nailed to the wooden wall upside down."

As James heard of this savage murder, he began to perspire and his face turned insipidly pallid. With a nervous voice, he asked, "Where on the grounds was this Mortimer executed?"

The baron looked darkly into the hearth's perishing embers, smiled grimly, and answered, "His very tomb is located on Wycliff Manor's southern tier, in a small cemetery next to the forest. It was not far from where his tomb now stands that he was rightfully executed."

"Nailed to a wall?" James asked, hands trembling.

"And why not?" the baron enquired.

The conversation ceased for a few moments before the baron mysteriously smiled at James, explaining, "You must understand, Mr. Asher. King Edward was a Saxon. And like all true Saxon nobles, within their minds, a Nation must always continue developing in a warlike state—to flourish from within.

"A true Saxon king does not subscribe to the notion that the motives for war should be to establish peace. For a country can only thrive during times of dire battles and conflicts. Only by a baptism of violence can a soldier's soul be truly tried and proven as a worthy candidate for the toils of bloodshed. Only then can he shed his blood on the field of honor as Woden did to appease the other gods of war. The tale of my people goes back to the days when the Norman Horde of France attacked the Britons who had villages here on this land in 1066.

"These noble and savage warriors brought the mighty spirits of Thor and Woden. And when the Englishman could offer no resistance, the Normans took their land with a fierce and wrathful determination to hold it until time's end."

Finishing his narrative, the baron reclined in his regal chair. By this time, the moon was hovering high in the western sky throwing long shadows upon the dining room floor. As James extinguished his already dead cigar, the baron stood to say good night before leaving James alone with his fears and the terrible products of his haunted imagination.

From a grave outside, a soul moaned in anguish and the rumbling of thunder could be heard in the distance. From one of the halls, a grandfather clock chimed twice. James got up from his fireside chair, leaving the huge dining room to attain the relative privacy of his bed chamber.

On his way up the stairs to the third floor he beheld a terrible vision. What appeared to be some sort of a ghost appeared from nowhere. A half-translucent specter, it was completely devoid of a body. Only a dark, tattered raiment covered the wraith, whose soul was black and transparent. Its airy hands attacked James, wrapping them around his neck so powerfully that James couldn't breathe. Although the face of the being was as black as its body, its outline was discernible in the moonlight streaming from an adjacent window.

James could feel his legs losing strength as his blood flow became weaker and weaker. The ghost continued to wrap its grip ever tighter around James' neck. His eyes became glassy, filling with tears. His mind darkened as he looked up to witness a spider's web dissolve before his eyes. The ghost snickered madly, sneering as James lost all consciousness, sinking to the steps of the staircase.

Some twenty minutes later, James regained consciousness in the fury of a violent rainstorm on one of the edges of the manor's roof. No ghost was to be seen. James surmised he had been carried to the mansion's roof by that dreadful spirit and had been left abandoned by the ghost to die.

The rainstorm raged as James struggled to stand. Straightening his legs, James fell on the roof's slippery precipice just barely plunging to his death. Regaining his balance, he moved toward the structure's center between the towers of the manor. Proceeding to walk along the roof in the dark, James somehow maneuvered himself over a ceiling window. As he did, the window broke under his body's weight and James fell through the now broadly open cavity in the roof along with a shower of glass to the hard floor of a room not far from his bed chamber. Landing head first with arms outstretched he again lost all awareness.

James lay unconscious and prostrate for close to an hour below the aperture of the roof in a widening pool of rain soaking his body. When he awoke, his clothing was drenched, and his head was ached terribly. He began to sob.

That's when he heard, once more, the malevolent laughter of Beelzebub from the graveyard far below.   ☩

Chapter Nineteen
The Gallery

As time progressed at Wycliff Manor, James
Asher, Junior became increasingly afraid. Although
it was now the final month of spring in the southwestern
part of England, the very halls of the Manor had
inexplicably become more wintry and dry. The joy and
happiness James had known in his former life had
completely disappeared since he became an inhabitant of
the capacious and haunted vile palace.

The whirlpool of mysterious and horrible happenings
profoundly shook James' mind, emotions, and nervous
equilibrium. The influence of the huge bastion and its
haunted grounds had forced James into a self-imposed
state of seclusion. On this third night of June, more than
three weeks had gone by since his arrival at the mansion,
and James had concluded that the entire place and its
surroundings were the origins of a multifarious brew of
malicious evils.

To occupy his tortured mind with thoughts other than beings of evil, James looked for any kind of escape. He would often spend considerable time after his nightly dinner talks with the baron gazing at the many portraits of royal figures in the darkly lit hall. James could not help but notice the incredible resemblance between the countenance of Baron Von Drake and the pigmented face of King Edward III. The King's face seemed almost alive hanging on the wall in the long, dark corridor.

One night after supper, the baron found James gazing at the King's portrait with keen interest.

"Ah! You have found the noble King! He constructed this very house using the hands of loyal slaves. And these chambers, halls, roofs, and walls were his home when he was away from Windsor Castle. Above all else, he was a great and courageous warrior. In 1337, he extended great territorial gains for the empire by conquering the French at Crécy-en-Ponthieu in Picardy, where he fought the Hundred Years' War. And what was more—he never knew fear.

"His father had his royal titles unjustly stripped, due to the criminal Roger Mortimer, so King Edward III took back his crown by nailing that scoundrel Mortimer to a wall, as I told you. Such days of merciless courage have sadly died away. It is said that King Edward III was buried at Westminster Abbey when he died.

"But I happen to know quite differently… " the baron said with mysterious intonation.

As the baron continued speaking, the King's deep,

blue gaze peered into James' eyes from the large, painted canvass. The striking similarity between the two men was profound. When the baron formally excused himself (as he did almost every night), he left James alone in the hall.

Several evenings later, after spending the dusky hours of the dying day drinking cognac in the company of the baron, James could not help but notice the baron's new elaborate attire.

It was quite different from the accouterments the baron usually wore. This night, the baron donned a splendid gold shirt clad with various aristocratic metals and vertical frills fashioned from the most regal fabrics. Baron Von Drake's waistcoat was of the most costliest attire, a fine gilded silk. The baron was also brandishing a conspicuous bronze metal with the letter "E" royally engraved upon his lapel. Upon noticing this curious emblem, James laid his empty glass of brandy on the table before him. For unknown reasons, the baron abruptly left James alone in the dining room after a courtly bow.

James bolted from his chair and ran to behold the portrait of King Edward III in the hall. This time there could be no mistake. For in the portrait, King Edward III wore the same attire that the baron had worn the previous night—down to the last detail. James stared open-eyed at the painted "E" on the King's lapel. The "E" was engraved in a sangria-hued red upon a regal lily-white background—the exact same emblem the baron had been wearing. The characteristics of every detail in the painted attire of King Edward III were the same as the baron's, manifesting not the slightest deviation. For the first time, James read the dust-covered inscription beneath the painting—it had previously escaped his notice being on the left-hand corner of the frame.

King Edward the III at Windsor Castle, 1352.

James stepped three paces from the wall displaying the enigmatic object fearing his reason had become unhinged. Exacerbating his unstable condition, James saw a thinly painted inscription on the portrait's lower right-hand corner which read, *John Kenneth Dwight, Wycliff Manor, 3 January 1353.*

This reference was ostensibly related to the man who hung himself in the attic, leaving the letter behind. The unfortunate artist had evidently commenced working on the painting at Windsor Castle yet had finished it at Wycliff Manor one year later, just prior to hanging himself.

Believing the two men, Baron William Von Drake and King Edward III, were one and the same, for the first time in his life, James Asher, Junior felt the sensation of profound and complete hopelessness along with a distant but growing feeling of utter panic.

Suddenly, a mysterious rumbling seemed to shake the very foundations of the entire house. In response to the thunderous quake, the portrait of King Edward III rattled on the wall. Before it fell in a moment's flash, the painted face of King Edward III became animated, as alive as any being living upon earth. The mouth of the painted king spoke with the voice of a true fallen soul.

"Damn you, James!"

With that, the casing of the entire portrait fell, its antique glass crashing into countless pieces, along with its frame, on the hardwood floor in the hall.

The earth continued to quake, causing the entire manor to shake. Then, from the other end of the passage, from the rear of the abysmal, baneful, black hall, a fiendish laughter resounded.

As the earthquake became more intense, the laughter grew. Only this laughter did not originate from the mouth of any ghost or brute. Nor did it emanate from the animated spirit of a dead human. Once more, it gushed forth from the mocking sneer of the netherworld's demonic prince.

James bolted to his room and lay on his bed in a cold sweat, his mind tortured with visceral nightmares.

Somewhere below, a dog was lamentably wailing. Although the quake had stopped, wild gushes of wind were now rushing through open windows, rattling the panes. A slow, creeping mist entered through the casements, flowing down to the hard, wooden floor, billowing like an amorphous spirit across the room.

From the far side of James' room, a firm and loud knock rang out upon the chamber door. Startled and bewildered, James sat on his bed, silent and motionless, refusing to inquire who was knocking. He could feel his heart pulsating like a mallet through his temples as he listened with all his being.

After a momentary pause, which to James seemed

endless, another knock upon the door (much louder than the first) was succeeded by a pounding, this time moving the door in its frame. More outright violent poundings upon the portal followed, each louder and more violent than the previous.

James exclaimed in a furious fit of rage, "Who the devil are you? What do you want of me?"

A dreamy and ghostly voice replied, "Oh, James, have you forgotten me?"

The voice was familiar to James. It was the voice of a woman he knew some time ago.

"Do you still love the ocean, James? Is your ship still afloat? Do you still love me? Did you really believe I would never return?"

The ghostly voice ceased to speak. James knew what these cryptic statements referred to, as well as the woman addressing him. He rose and dashed like lightning from his bed to the door with agonizing anticipation. Yet the moment he opened the door, no one was there—an empty, dark hallway met his troubled gaze.

Beads of perspiration were trailing down James' face as he stood on the threshold, exhausted and terrified, unable or unwilling to close the door. As he gazed blindly into a faraway recess of the hall, he heard another voice echoing from the end of the long, dark corridor. This menacing and malicious voice had a masculine tone.

"Death awaits you, James, and hell arrives with your death. And I will forever rejoice to watch you burn." ✙

Chapter Twenty
The Vaults

Upon hearing the voice of humanity's ultimate enemy, James knew that Wycliff Manor was a literal microcosm of hell. Now, nothing existed in his mind but escape from the accursed place by any possible means.

Flying down the circular stair through the main foyer, James ran to front entrance. To his utter despair, the entry was again bolted solidly from the outside. No matter how hard he pulled, he could not budge the door one iota. At last he collapsed, hopeless, discouraged, and dazed, into a dusty, old, embroidered chair next to the door.

After about twenty minutes, feeling a slight, soft breeze, James lifted his head to gaze toward the right of the main entrance. For the first time, he beheld a slender opening in the wall among a small library furnished with old books. Any possible means out of the manor for James was a risk worth pursuing—even if he wasn't sure where his pursuit would lead. Squeezing through the slender opening, James found himself in a dark passage leading to another long hall that descended into what James surmised was a portion of the mansion's lowest level. He was headed toward the manor's keep.

With no lights of any kind, James removed a candelabra from one of the walls and lit its candles with a book of matches he carried in his pocket. As he did, the wall clad with books behind him, which procured the only opening to the hallway, suddenly and mysteriously slammed shut. James was now in utter darkness, as the candles he had lit immediately went out from the gush of wind caused by the violent closing of the opening.

Having used the last of his matches, James was now entombed in total blackness. A ghostly voice emanated from the end of the light-less hall with a fatal, menacing tone.

"Mortimer! Mortimer!"

James knew who Mortimer was, the murdered despot killed by King Edward III (who had accosted James), but James could not understand how Mortimer man could be related to himself in any way.

Again the ghostly voice spoke, "Mortimer, Mortimer!"

James replied in a fit of mad rage, "My name is Asher! You wretched wraith!"

The voice didn't answer; instead, in a flash, a dagger was thrown upon the floor at James' feet. The chandelier above James' head suddenly lit without source of any natural means. James looked to his right and noticed an inscription carved on a wide slab of wood hanging over the entrance of what appeared to be an ancient series of burial vaults.

All ye who enter here abandon all hope.

A trail of roaches and rats clamored across the mold-ridden entrance floor. As James ventured into the dim light of the catacombs, a putrid odor filled the thick, dusty air. Progressing within, he found rusty metal chains and fragments of skeletons lying within splintered crates. Finally, he came upon two conspicuously isolated crypts.

On the left was a large stone crypt on which the words were written.

Here lies the eternal resting place of King Edward III.

To the right of the sarcophagus was an equally imposing burial chamber upon which was written:

Here lies the eternal resting place of Philippa of Hainault, the wife of King Edward III.

James advanced toward the king's crypt with a slow and cautious pace. Seeing stone coffin lid had been deposed; he looked down to inspect the coffin. The death chamber was empty.

Below the words of King Edward III was engraved, *Baron William Charles Von Drake*. The death house of the king's wife was also vacant, yet below her name was another, *Susan Margret Bennet*.

Without warning, the baron appeared behind James, "Us death walkers need not sleep, Mr. Mortimer!"

"My name is Asher! You gruesome old phantom!" James replied with virulent rage and despair. "Stay away from me! Or you will die a second time!"

The baron explained, "You are one of the last two Mortimers living, and you will never leave this house alive! I refuse to allow a remnant of his seed to walk upon the soil of my world!"

James ran screaming from the vaults, passing the baron and escaping through the slender exit, now mysteriously open, into the hallway. Panicked, he ran up the stone stairways across the long passage back to the main floor.

"If I can not escape this horrible prison of ghosts and demons, then at least I must defend myself!" he spoke aloud.

He headed toward the western tower's small room in the attic where he had found the letter written by the painter. This time, at the bottom of the same chest in which James had first found the suicide letter, he discovered another. This one seemed ages old, torn at the edges, and mostly crumpled. Yet, the handwriting seemed fairly new.

The Confessions of a King... I write this testament in honor of my angelic benefactor, Satan, my prince of light. As I approached my death, as did my wife, I summoned the diabolic forces. They came to me, promising us eternal life in exchange for our absolute alliance.

And so my wife and I have been living as regal souls for seven-hundred years. My final task is to utterly wipe the last two corrupted souls from this earth who are descended from Roger Mortimer, the murderer who took my father's life. I know from the demons that one is an American who calls himself Asher. I must bring him here to dispose of his criminal lungs, forever stopping them from breathing.

The second and last Mortimer living is a Scot who calls himself Simon. He is another cowardly soul who poses as a sort of businessman. He dwells up north in the region of Edinburgh. He, too, shall be brought here.

Only then will Philippa and I know true peace. She will lure both men here, and at the appropriate time, we will do away with them, one by one. May the last traces of their tainted blood be blotted from our universe!

And thus the letter ended. James cast it on the floor after crushing it with a maddened fist shouting, "My God!"

That very night, as James fell asleep in that same attic room, the door to the small chamber slowly and softly opened with enough breeze to cause James to open his eyes. He beheld a most beautiful woman. Her hair was black and her eyes brown; her lips were velvet-like and redder than a carmine-hued blossom.

She opened her dark red lips and slowly, in a seductive whisper, spoke. "Hello, my dear cousin. I am Susan, returned to greet you. Welcome to my house… " With soft confidence, she moved toward James, smiling a strange and visible hunger in her eyes. Her gaze was intense and sable. James believed she resembled the animated corpse in the graveyard he had witnessed. Only now, she appeared in all ways most fair.

Taking another step toward James, Susan produced the sound of a tinkling bell from a golden ankle bracelet she wore. With deceptive grace in the gleaming white moonlight, she spoke again with a smooth, delicate murmur, "Love me, James." Looking at James admiringly, she bewitchingly whispered, "Kiss me, my fair cousin."

James' head seemed to spin as if his mind were being brought under some Orphic spell. Yet he did not kiss her. He agonized in a state of bewildered hesitation sensing an impending danger.

Susan became impatient, "Will you not oblige me?" She spoke slowly with the falsely attractive inflection of a true Siren, "Do I not appear to your eyes fairer than any rose, James?"

Every syllable which flowed from her mouth placed James deeper and deeper under her potent sensual spell. Her spell was so forceful James found it almost impossible to resist—as if Susan was summoning up a dark, undeniable, and enigmatic power. James felt completely enslaved by the mystical control Susan now had over him.

Determined, she took another step forward. Liberally parting her lips, she begged him for a kiss in the streaming silver moonlight. Reluctantly lacing his hands around the long, dark tresses of Susan's head, James impulsively kissed her. Yet as he did he tasted a strange and repulsive bitterness on her lips.

Susan continued to attempt to influence James further with yet another buss. Yet her power over James was fading as James was sobering from the sway of her demonic trance.

Hanging on the red brick wall behind Susan's figure hung a tall, vertical mirror which James just noticed. A moment after Susan tried to kiss him the second time, he saw a long, sharp knife hidden in Susan's left hand behind her back in the mirror. He immediately and violently threw her from him and ran for his life to study one flight down.

Entering the medium-sized room, he locked the door from which he entered and hid underneath a large, old, dust-ridden sofa. An extreme state of fear and panic beset him which he imagined no amount of time could ever assuage.   ✟

Chapter Twenty-One
The Crypts

Two nights later, at about dusk, James awoke late in a small room across the hallway from his own. At roughly midnight on the previous evening, James had abandoned his dismal room out of sheer loathing for the insufferable place.

When he had first entered the small room, he found it to be a sort of study. The only furniture was that of a plain, rather large desk and a wooden chair made of mahogany. Strange to James was the fact that not one window was to be seen in the dusty, old room. The lack of windows was for the simple reason that the chamber was situated in the center of the mansion, far from all outer walls, on the Manor's highest floor between its four teeming towers.

This study was particularly ominous, as if a merciless and nebulous crime had taken place a long time ago. Upon waking, James pervaded every portion of the chamber keenly with peering gazes before collapsing into the mahogany chair to recline in a state of deep fatigue.

As sleep began to overcome him, James felt, as he stretched his legs, something sizable lying behind and beneath the desk. Then James heard a voice from under the desk say in a ghostly tone, with all the tenses of anguish:

"Do you know what happened here?"

James was stunned. The sudden, unexpected voice thrilled him with a timeless quality that made James quiver.

"I was betrayed!" the voice said with a vile resentment. "Do you still not know where you are? Do you still not know who summoned you here? Do you still not know who resides here?"

James asked a simple question, which could only have for its answer something terrible. "Who are you?"

"My name is Mortimer," the thing replied. "I was not killed outside when I was nailed to the wall! I was stabbed in my back from behind in this very room in the very chair in which you now sit!"

Next James felt something wet behind his back and twisted his body to discover a pool of blood streaming down the rear of the chair. With a dreadful fear that no words can describe, James looked down to behold behind the desk an outstretched hand on the bare wood floor. It was a human hand, the kind of hand that one sees countless times in the course of one's life. Yet although this hand was trembling, it possessed an all-pervasive deathly pallor, for it was the hand of Mortimer, the dead.

Just as James attempted to rise in a state of desperate terror, he found that he could not move. It was as though an otherworldly force, a malevolent and occult power, prevented James from standing. A baneful energy was blocking his escape.

The dead man spoke again. Only this time in a more grim and raspy manner. "One and one do not make two here. One and one make one!"

As James heard this enigmatic statement, the cold, gray walls of the ancient study seemed to close in upon him. In less than a moment, the tortured voice emanating from the being underneath the desk uttered a mere thirteen syllables which chilled every ounce of blood in James' body. It spoke once more, for the last time, slowly and with a loud fervor. With the despairing tone of a soul beyond all hope, the voice cried out in a way that was painful to hear, "For the Baron and King Edward III are one and the same!"

A bolt of lightning suddenly crashed through the ceiling illuminating the entire room as if the damning rays of a hellish sun lit up the chamber employing all the powers of accursed alchemy. Next came a series of pounding thunder blasts that swayed the foundations of the house to its very cornerstone. After these rumbling blasts, the unholy incandescent glow lighting the chamber did not fade but instead became brighter.

And to James' cruel shock, to the right of the desk in one corner of the study, the figure of Baron Von Drake appeared out of the former darkness.

The baron looked into James' eyes with an evil hatred and began to laugh. James became overwhelmed by the horror and fell head forward onto the desk. As he did, all the light in the study died and James sank from the chair unconscious.

The second week of June had come and gone, and the wan, lurid sun had expired beyond the ancient graveyard in the western sky. Another night swept over the somber and lordly estate like a vast and loathsome curtain of impending death.

Although James had frequently wandered through the various spaces and chambers within the enormous house, he had done so primarily to find an ulterior exit from the manor as the main door on the first floor remained firmly bolted.

On this night, James avoided the company of the baron and the dining room. As he descended the main staircase, an organ began playing carnival music from somewhere in the monolithic house. In each one of the fortification's towers, bells were loudly clanging. James finally reached the first floor of the house, desperately searching for an exit.

Trying once again, he pulled at the knob on the titanic entry of the ancient door and found it once more securely locked from the outside. He became alarmed as he heard slow approaching footsteps descending the circular staircase.

James turned round to behold the features of Phillipa, who called herself Susan, brandishing her long, silver knife. Her eyes were red and betrayed all the intentions of a savage murderer. Propelled by sheer terror, James abruptly ran down another flight of stone steps to the lowest level of the bastion. Quickly walking down another grim encasement, he found a series of dark tunnels.

Upon further observation, he realized he was in the midst of yet another different labyrinth of medieval catacombs. He continued down one of the corridors with trepidation, and without much effort, came upon an antiquated and murky dungeon.

Within this cell were four skeletal corpses lying on the stone floor of the age-old prison. Each cadaver was chained to the walls with thick metal fetters. As James looked closely at the details of the gulag, he heard the murderous strides of Phillipa approaching. She was on fire with a passion to kill James with her long sharp knife; nothing less would do.

Unexpectedly from behind, James felt the strong grasp of the baron's hands upon his shoulders. The whole of the baron's demeanor had become a grisly caricature of his former self. His countenance was limpid; his eyes were glossy, betraying all the pallor of the dead. Holding James in place, the baron smiled as Phillipa approached ever closer, saber in hand.

Turning James toward him, the baron spoke in a despotic, tyrannical voice, "This is your end, Mister Mortimer. There is nowhere to run."

Now a mere two feet away from James' back, Phillipa let out an appalling, repulsive laugh. Preparing to use her dagger, she sneered at James.

At once James clenched his right hand to make a firm fist and struck the baron's face with a mighty blow. The powerful impact bludgeoned the baron, and he fell backward releasing James from his iron clasp.

Phillipa raised her knife high into the air and struck at James' back with a fierce and swift downward clap. Just missed the blow of the steely blade by less than half an inch, James eyed the door and fled up the staircase from which he had descended to attain the manor's main floor.   ✙

Chapter Twenty-Two
The Forest

Pacing the floor of the great manor's entry, James was pensively musing how to escape. Hearing a rustling of trees outside the great windows, he looked through to behold a darkly luminous figure slowly walking along the lawn, devoid of a body yet not a ghost. The dismal entity stopped to look at James, who felt a shiver as he witnessed the specter point a ghastly finger directly at him. The figure then began laughing, first mildly, then with vigor.

James screamed at the evil, mysterious being, "What do you want with me?"

"Much! For you have long betrayed the One who made you in His image. You and I shall forevermore be companions, Mr. Asher. Although you might not care for my company—nor my eternal retinue!"

Seeing and hearing this, James flew to the spiral stone stairs for the sake of his life to descend several flights. For the first time since his arrival, he had entered the extreme southern part of the house.

A sort of chapel with a tall stained glass window positioned close to the floor stood before him. If James could break the glass, its frame was large enough for him to crawl through and perhaps escape.

As he looked for a tool with which to strike the glass, he heard approaching footsteps. Turning his head, he saw the dead woman, Philippa, who had called herself Susan, quickly coming toward him still clutching the butcher's knife in her pale, chalky hand.

James' eye caught a glint from a monumental metal globe on a heavy walnut desk near the window. Seizing the circular object, he thrust it with great force. The stained glass crashed and splintered falling to the courtyard floor below. At the same time, James felt the cold metal from the blade the dead woman held. The potentially fatal blow just missed the core of his back, cutting through his shirt, scraping his skin.

With tremendous strength he wasn't sure he had, James lifted the vast desk high above his head and screamed, "Damn you!" and brought the whole of the massive piece down upon the head of the dead woman. The immense walnut desk fell to the floor splintering into several pieces. An excessive amount of blood rained down the face of the deceased specter.

James leaped to the base of the now open casement and jumped five feet to the alabaster floor of the square below. The night air was violent with strong winds and James could see the many illuminated stars in the wild firmament. Beyond the courtyard lay the dark, lugubrious forest.

As James approached the wood, the silvery orbs above suddenly became almost completely cloaked in a thick, mysterious mist—as if the stars did not exist. He felt an ominous presence living in the dreary forest and sensed that a profound danger awaited him in the darkness of the throng of decrepit trees. Knowing he could not return to the hell of Wycliff Manor, he ran into the forest at a furious speed without delay.

The floor of the shaded wood was covered with a sheet of dead leaves, which the wild breezes lifted and scattered in a godless, swirling, meandering dance. James tripped over stumps of dead trees and briars, sliding on the wet grass from the previous night's rain.

From the dimly lit forest, appearing in all his demonic horror, the dark, angelic figure whom James now knew to be Lucifer was quickly approaching.

"You fool, you! Thinking that your image and likeness bearing its resemblance to the One I Hate could ever make me suffer you to be with Him!?

"Do you recall Michelle Hull?!"

James Asher, Junior, while still a graduate student at Harvard University, was a member of the Edgartown Yacht Club on Martha's Vineyard. He would often pass his free time in the summer leisurely off the shores of New England in the cradle of the sea under the warmth of the sun. At twenty-four, James was earning his master's degree. During this time, he had a girlfriend with whom he had became intimately involved for a few years, Michelle Hull.

Michelle was a comely though shy young woman and a Harvard student. When James first met her at school, he imagined he had found paradise in another person's spirit. Yet, two years later, he could barely stand to be in her company. Michelle was primarily a needy and clingy brand of person. Yet, although Michelle was faulted in several ways, she possessed a true goodness that dwelled in her heart. This goodness reigned within her being as her most beautiful and defining characteristic. As time went by, though, that very same goodness became to James the most tangible symbol of what and whom he hated the most—his Creator and Redeemer.

For although James had professed fervent atheism since his youth, he knew only too well in his heart and mind that God did indeed exist. Furthermore, he blamed the almighty for each and every unfortunate happening in his life, making God, in James' view, a cruel and eternal enemy, a tyrannical deity. And since Michelle embodied the goodness of many of God's traits, she also became a mortal enemy to James in a relatively short period of time during their first year together.

By killing Michelle, in James' evil heart and psyche, he could possibly detract from God's place those traits which, to James, were the composites of the being he hated the most—namely God himself. As James had become more distant and utterly consumed with a fiery hatred for Michelle, she began leaving pieces of her jewelry at his studio flat and on his newly purchased yacht as an excuse to see him again, not knowing that her life was in imminent danger.

The disdain James harbored for Michelle reached such a profound intensity beyond all reason that James Asher, Junior, for the first time in his life, decided to commit a heartless murder.

As time passed, James, in his hateful mind, believed he had no choice but to kill Michelle in the most brutal and literal sense of the term. Ceasing to see Michelle was not enough—he felt a savage and insatiable need to mercilessly and completely obliterate every remnant of her being from the planet. Michelle's similarity to God's good nature was too hateful not to destroy her in a swift and utter way.

James was an excellent seaman, and by the time he had finished training as a master mariner, he could easily navigate the expensive state-of-the-art yacht through all water and weather conditions.

One night in late July, after James had acquired his master's degree, with a grim and solemn purpose, James took his vessel with Michelle on board far out upon the open sea. He ferried his luxurious yacht beyond the final land barrier separating the mainland from the Atlantic Ocean toward Nantucket Sound. On this particular night, neither Michelle's friends nor acquaintances knew she would be with James. James had made certain of this.

The night air was chilly for July, and the dwarf was vacant save for James' pearly white forty-five-foot yacht. James had ensured no one observed her presence on the boat nor the vessel departing from the dock.

He drove the powerful craft quietly and steadily eastward for about an hour. At a certain obscure point far out at sea, he slowly turned off the engine. The long boat rocked gently in the swaying billows, gleaming like a horizontal pearl in the unobscured moonlight.

A dire, moral blackness entered James' heart as he contemptuously gazed at Michelle lounging on the ship's deck. She wore a long, fashionable pink coat over a plain white sweater, and was sitting on a lavender-tinted cushion, reclining on rounded rails, drinking a glass of fine Chardonnay.

He watched her enjoy the thick scent of the salty, saline zephyrs. They filled her lungs as though she were betrothed to a god. Indeed, she felt engaged with the kind of handsome Superman one finds in the ancient Grecian tales of Adonis.

From the crow's nest, the stars above looked small to the eye. They were almost unnoticeable as the sea was so calm that James could hardly tell where the surface of the water divided the surf from the sky. He descended from his perch, he looked down at Michelle with intense disdain. Producing a pair of newly bought binoculars, James investigated the waters for close to a mile around the ship. No other vessel was in sight, and by this time, the yacht was far from all land. He slowly walked to the stern of the boat where Michelle was sitting.

She looked up at James with a sultry smile. As she opened her mouth to utter a content and amorous phrase of endearment, James, with mighty hands and all his strength, wrapped his fingers with a lion's grip around her pale, white neck. She began convulsing and kicking in a futile manner as her face turned a monstrous, dark blue. Her nose began to bleed. James' hands were as a vice made of steel and he wavered not a moment strangling his lover.

In a matter of seconds, Michelle's movements became completely still. Tears profusely streamed from her ruddy eyes until her breathing had ceased.

Her life was no more.

James looked on with intense delight witnessing her corpse awkwardly fall to the ship's floor. With calm premeditation, he walked a few paces to port to retrieve a heavy metallic chair he had placed in a dark and inconspicuous corner of the vessel's stern very early that morning, prior to dawn.

Using a thick, tightly wound rope, he proceeded to join Michelle and the chair in a bond so strong that neither time nor the elements could ever begin to part them. Once the many knots were firmly fastened, James' final act was to toss the corpse and chair into the fathomless depths of the black Atlantic.

The foul cargo gleamed for a momentary flash of time in the naked moonlight before sinking wholly and abruptly one mile to the bottom of the ocean's floor.

In the accursed forest, Satan mocked, "That's right, James Asher. Michelle escaped my hands. But your fate is eternal fire! And in a moment's time, you shall be in my realm! Without an end, beyond all hope forever!"

The complexion of James' face morphed into that of a pallid statue. He flew deeper into the woods at top speed to escape Wycliff Manor, Susan, and the Devil.

Sprinting into the shadows of the wild forest, James began hyperventilating as he tumbled over throngs of briars, tall reeds, and bushes. He could hear the laughter of the being who called herself Susan rapidly approaching from behind. In his utter panic, he began losing speed in his stride.

With the quickness of a dark-winged angel, Susan quickly caught up to James and, in a moment's time, was behind him. She raised her lethal weapon high and plunged her knife deep into James' back.

A painful sensation ripped through James' spine as he toppled over, down upon the grass. Motionless and prostrate, James' head violently slammed hard upon a stone. As he tried to focus, he witnessed his hands pass transparently through the tall, yellow reeds before him, yet he could not feel the reeds at all.

Then, rising like a spring, James arose and again raced through the forest, believing he might escape. Yet as he did so, he felt an entirely new and profound terror rush throughout his being, a strange, amorphous, ethereal sensation—as though he had passed into a completely different realm. James had passed through an intangible veil between two realms of existence—one of life and the other of death. Looking back to where he had fallen, with inexpressible horror, James beheld his corpse lying motionless upon a large stone with the knife lodged in its back, blood flowing from what was once his mouth.

Standing behind James' corpse, Beelzebub, the Satanic angel, the Devil himself, that imperious, proud, and ancient dragon, spoke, "So, you thought you could get away with murder, did you, James?"

An enigmatic force threw James' disembodied spirit violently against one of the accursed oak trees. An invisible link of intangible chains secured his soul against the base of the wide oak's thick trunk. James could see, in the breezy leaf-barren forest, the illuminated, hateful, demonic figure of Lucifer swiftly approaching his imprisoned spirit.

The final dim remnants of the nebulous moonlight streaming through creaking branches of trees long ago expired lit James' corpse. Satan pointed down to a dark, round bog laying on the edge of the forest, immediately before the tree to which James was a prisoner.

James looked down to witness the bog begin turning rapidly counterclockwise swallowing all in its surrounding area. The black, cold, briny soil morphed into a profoundly rich, scarlet red. And as his eyes followed the now brightly lit tornado beneath his feet, James could feel an ineffable, extreme, and unearthly heat rising from the vortex.

The Devil looked on and laughed with hellish delight

as James, wailing, was seized and swallowed by the torrid pit, never to be seen upon the earth again.

The very next evening, a traveler from Scotland knocked on the great, imposing old door of Wycliff Manor. In a few minutes, the door was slowly opened by Baron Von Drake, greeting the newly arrived visitor who had never seen the manor before.

"Please allow me to introduce myself. I am Baron William Charles Von Drake. You must be Master Simon Mortimer. Unfortunately, my servants are away due to a family bereavement. But please, do come in. For the night air is cold and unforgiving, and you must be very hungry…"

Meanwhile, up comes the moon; The park
Lights up the mist which clings to the bark
Among the many demons, dreaming in the dark. ✞

About the Author

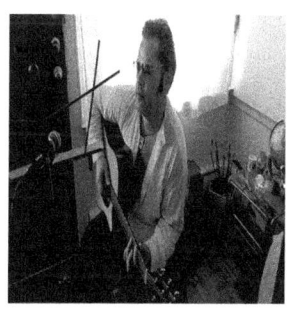

John Lars Zwerenz (1969 -) was born and raised in New York City. After extensive travel, by the time his first widely published volume of poetry, "Selected Poems," was released in 2011, Zwerenz was established as a prolific writer and journalist. His literary genres include verse, fiction, articles, anthologies, and academic essays.

In 2014, Zwerenz became the official poetry writer for the internationally published print arts publication *Emage Magazine International* and went on to publish ten more books of verse and two novellas.

Among his later works are *Eternal Verse* (2013); *Elysian Meadows* (2017); *Mystic Wines* (2018); and *The House on Marble Hill* (2019). In 2020, Zwerenz's entire poetic catalog, *The Complete Anthology*, which includes *Cathedrals in the Rain*, was released.